W9-BRO-854

RUBY'S
HUMANS

RUBY

RUBY'S HUMANS

A DOG'S-EYE MEMOIR

TOM ADRAHTAS

CLEARWATER I FL I USA

For information, contact Kunati Inc., Book Publishers in Canada.
USA: 13575 58th Street North, Suite 200, Clearwater, FL 33760-3721 USA
Canada: 75 First Street, Suite 128, Orangeville, ON L9W 5B6 CANADA.
E-mail: info@kunati.com.

F I R S T   E D I T I O N

Designed by Kam Wai Yu
Persona Corp. | www.personaco.com

ISBN 978-1-60164-188-5   EAN 9781601641885
Non-Fiction/Pet/Dogs/Memoire

Published by Kunati Inc. (USA) and Kunati Inc. (Canada).
Provocative. Bold. Controversial.™

h t t p : / / w w w . k u n a t i . c o m

Library of Congress Cataloging-in-Publication Data

Adrahtas, Tom, 1955-
Ruby's humans : a dog's-eye memoir / Tom Adrahtas. -- 1st ed.
    p. cm.
Summary: "An irreverent, dog's-eye view of humans in which Ruby heaps
scorn on our species and the popular culture we create, saving her sharpest
barbs for the often neurotic relationships we form with members of her
kind"--Provided by publisher.
ISBN 978-1-60164-188-5
1. Dogs--Humor. 2. Human-animal relationships--Humor. I. Title.
PN6231.D68A37 2009
818'.602--dc22
                                    2008056143

DEDICATION

In loving memory of Panayota Adrahtas,
beloved Yia Yia

TA

In loving memory of Leika,
the canine hero,
who PRECEDED humans into space.

R

ACKNOWLEDGEMENTS

I extend my deepest appreciation to those who helped instill in me the love of dogs, beginning with my late grandmother, Panayota Adrahtas. Also to my uncle, the late Al Borowski, the perfect master to Duchess, Lady, Tia, Gia, and Duchess II, and his wife, my aunt Ginny Borowski who's kept the tradition and his memory alive by spoiling Lady II and Duchess III more than any other dogs who've walked the face of the Earth.

My gratitude also to the selfless workers of the shelters throughout the world, whose quiet dedication is the lifeline for so many creatures who live only to share their love.

As always, to my friends who are my chosen family and fellow dog lovers; Gregg, Mike, Ronnie, Matt, Billy, Kelly and Mandy, Jim and Diane, Vi, Marie, Teach and Shannon, Hallzy and Nicole, The Teglia family, the Morris family, Ken Frost and Eugenia Frost, and the Wallaces. Also to Eve Cooper, to whom I owe more than I can ever repay.

Special gratitude to Nancy Rosenfeld, who took a chance meeting and to whom I owe an incalculable amount for the simple act of believing.

Special thanks to Amberly Schmidt for her wonderful photographs of Ruby.

And of course, to my Ruby. You will get an extra cookie for inspiring all of this.

T.A.

"I Know Why the Leashed Dog Howls"

by Ruby
(with Tom Adrahtas)

CONTENTS

FOREWORD

I have the most beautiful, most intelligent, most adorable dog in the world. As a matter of fact, I can say with little fear of rebuttal that she is the most beautiful, most intelligent, most adorable dog in the history of the world. That Bichon you have? Very nice. Your chocolate Lab, the one you so cleverly named Mousse? A terrific dog, I'm sure. And you, the one whose mixed breed appeared on Letterman? Very impressed with her agility.

I know that every one of you reading this book has had those moments of weakness where you think *your* dog is the best one ever.

I want you to know that I understand.

I understand your need to *think* your dog is special, and I'm big enough to acknowledge and politely nod my approval at how unique your loving buddy is. But that still does not make him or her the most beautiful, most intelligent, most adorable dog in the world. My dog is. I am not biased when I stake that claim as fact, because it is fact. Indisputable. Provable. Verifiable.

How do I know?

I know.

Prove it, you say?

Do you believe there's a God?

Prove it.

Some things we just know. This, I know.

I won't state the obvious and lower the tone of this monologue by asking you to show me the book *your* dog wrote. That would be too easy. But since we're on the topic, my dog, the previously mentioned most beautiful, most intelligent, most adorable dog in the world, did write this one. I have to admit, I was more than a little flustered when I discovered what she was up to. There are many times throughout the text where I and my species are not cast in a light that is exactly glowing. But in the end, I think that you'll find the candor with which Ruby records her observations only lends to the book's credibility. I am proud of her work and grateful that she's opted to share her thoughts with the world.

If you're skeptical at all of either a dog's capacity to write, communicate in the human language, or offer valuable advice to humankind, I understand and cannot blame you. Your life's experience wouldn't have prepared you to be anything but skeptical. But that's because your dog is not the most beautiful, most intelligent, most adorable dog in the world.

Mine is.

Tom Adrahtas (Ruby's current human)

Outside of a dog, a book is man's best friend.
Inside of a dog, it's too dark to read.
Groucho Marx

CHAPTER ONE

ALL OF ME

(Note to Reader: Please accept my apology for the raw nature of the opening line that follows. My publisher insisted that I needed to "hook" your interest through any means possible, the more sensational the better. I fully realize that I'm appealing to the lowest common denominator by cooperating with this strategy, but I was helpless. I am, after all, a canine, and therefore operating at a distinct disadvantage when it comes to negotiating the content of the text. I would have much preferred opening with something more profound, à la "It was the best of times, it was the worst of times ..." Of course, that's been done to death, but you get my meaning.)

🐾 🐾 🐾

My name is Ruby, and I eat rabbit shit.

For this, I make no apology. I have no choice. It's just a part of who I am. I was, you see, the product of a mixed relationship that left me hardwired in certain areas of taste and habit. Mama was a beagle, Papa was a fox terrier. We hunt, we chase, we follow scents. Rabbits and squirrels are to us as meth is to trailer trash, as PAC money is to a politician, as hypocrisy is to TV evangelists.

And dear reader, make no judgments about my culinary peculiarities lest you be judged. Need I list some of what you people consider delicacies? Need I stress that for you, the following are tastes you indulge in strictly as a matter of choice?

Monkey brains? Bull testicles? Octopus? Sturgeon eggs? Stuffed intestines? Twinkies? Spam?

So don't begrudge me my epicurean eccentricity. Most of the rest of my human-enforced diet consists of dried beige and brown nuggets which I get every morning. Every single morning.

Every.

Single.

Morning.

Dried.

Beige.

Brown.

Nuggets.

Oh! Oh! Oh! But for dinner, I get the dried beige and brown nuggets *with* some unidentifiable chicken parts and brownish water that passes for gravy! Aren't I just sooooo lucky! Of course, I also get the occasional "dog" biscuits (I don't hear you call anything "human biscuits") when I'm especially subservient, and when I'm left alone for a long time, you deign to offer a nice beef-basted rawhide. Perhaps now you understand the urgency I feel when I'm out for a walk and lunge after those genetically-predetermined-as-desirable rabbit-passed morsels.

And why, you may be wondering, are I and my kind doomed to a life of such a bland and restricted diet?

Because some pet food company shill of a veterinarian was bought off by a brilliant young Madison Avenue ad exec to propagate the nonsense that "people food" is bad for canines. If people food were, as they conspired to have you believe, bad for us, people would have to buy more dog food!!! Brilliant! Evil genius, even! The side benefit for humans then is that if they are not sharing their food with "man's best friend," (and this food issue makes that seem like a very one-sided friendship indeed) there's more people food for you all to enjoy.

"Obesity is the number one killer of humans," chime the newsmen. "People don't get enough exercise," the papers proclaim. So what are people told? Getting a dog helps you get out and exercise more. "Get out there and walk the dog," they say. So people buy adorable Labs and put kerchiefs around their necks, and walk them for the exercise they provide, which makes both the canine and the human hungrier, which means the human buys more dog food and doesn't have to share any of his human food, which leaves more for the human to eat and counteracts the benefits of walking the canine in the first place.

So in order to actually enjoy the tastes of people food, we canines, reduced to the status of furry minstrels, are forced to resort to tricks. We sit up on our back legs, wave our paws in the air, roll over, shoot you all the cutest looks we can muster, only to be rewarded either with a scrap of pizza crust that would not tempt a starving Somalian, or with a stern, "Don't beg!"

Don't beg? Don't beg?

DON'T BEG??!!

What are we supposed to do? Here we are, creatures gifted with an extrasensory level of smell, dealing with aromas that are irresistible to the far inferior human senses, and we're supposed to pretend NOT to be interested in partaking of the feast? Another sign of your human frailties is your desire to have those around you act according to your expectations and comfort level as opposed to their nature. (Or perhaps there's a better reason it took you all so long to give women the vote, blacks equal rights, and are still dragging your feet on the gay marriage thing.) So of course we beg! If you all shared in the first place, we wouldn't have to beg. How about leaving us with just a shred of dignity? (And I'll address the other assaults on that dignity, like dressing us up in miniature clothes, forcing us to relieve ourselves in public, etc., a bit later.)

Wake up! Only the pet food companies benefit from this practice, people. Always look for motive. I learned that because when my current human leaves the house, he always leaves the TV on TNT. I know every episode of *Law and Order* by heart.

As I write this, I am four years old. That does not make me twenty-eight in human years. I mean, honestly, the arrogance some of you humans have. I'm simply four years old. If you need to explain to other humans that four dog years make me the equivalent of a twenty-eight-year-old human, knock yourself out. Although let me point out why this is wholly inaccurate. I do not:

-Have insurmountable credit card debt.

-Still live with my parents.

-Hang out at single bars desperately searching for a mate because I am constantly reminded that "the clock is ticking."

-Shop at Ikea.

-Yearn for the good old college fraternity/sorority days.

-Think when I reach the big 3-0 that life will cease.

As a four-year-old canine, I have already given birth to

five children (or "puppies" as you people call them), had my tubes tied (against my wishes, I might add—more about that later), spent time in a concentration camp (or "animal shelter" by your definition), and been forcibly moved away from my parents before I was four months old.

Experiencing half of that would put a twenty-eight-year-old human in thrice-weekly therapy sessions for life.

The first time I laid eyes on my current human, I was cowering in the back of a cage at Heartland Animal Shelter. The floor was chilled cement with a strategically placed drainage hole, the walls nothing but cheap chain-link fencing. I was allotted a silver bowl half filled with lukewarm water and a handful of kibble twice a day. You'd think I'd violated the Patriot Act. The only difference between this miserable hell-hole and Guantanamo Bay was that some of the prisoners there would eventually be set free without having being neutered as a condition of release.

I came to Heartland because of an act of kindness on the part of a human, the first real act of kindness I'd been shown by one of your species. He found me on the side of a road in Indiana. (As an aside, I'm a canine and even I don't get the purpose of Indiana.) Normally, I'd have never let him get close to me as humans scare the hell out of me. I'd earned that fear, having spent time in a house with a homo sapiens whose approach to teaching me acceptable behavior was to hit me hard and then harder. I'm a smart animal, a canine willing, even eager, to learn. Sit, stay, lie down, blah blah blah. I get it. I didn't need negative reinforcement. But that's what I got. Joan Crawford's daughter had it easy. The beatings left me human-shy. To this day, I flinch around any newcomers into my world. I'm not proud of that. I'm a beagle terrier mix after all, cute as hell. Little kids run up to me wanting to play, adults tell my current human how adorable I am. And how do I react to this wonderfully complimentary attention?

I cower.

But that's the legacy of an abusive home, a reminder to any of you reading this of what you leave in your wake when you use violence as a teaching tool. No doubt in my mind that if someone will do it to a canine, they'll do it to a fellow human too. Some, like me, and I assume some humans as well, react by withdrawing. But there are others out there, dogs and humans both, who react far differently. Some meet violence with violence. Real Old Testament stuff.

Either way, not a very good approach.

Anyway, I managed to escape my first human. I was just over a year old, and his offspring, the mini-humans or "minis" as we canines refer to them, (who were cute by your standards, but as irresponsible as he was) left me in the yard a little longer than they should have. My plans for escape started innocently enough. I could smell a squirrel on the other side of the fence, and almost by accident, extended my left paw out towards the base of the fence. When I scraped at the fence, the dirt beneath it moved. I did it again, and more dirt pulled away.

Hmmmm.

I repeated the motion, and the smell got stronger, more alluring. I began to dig quicker, and I saw just a glint of light between the soft soil and the base of the fence.

Double hmmmm.

Then I heard the screen door slide open, and my first human called me back into the house. I could only hope against hope that he wouldn't notice my little excavation. I knew that whatever was on the other side had to be better than where I was living. There was more than a squirrel on the other side of that fence; there was hope (and Mr. Obama just taught us how powerful that emotion can be). Back in the human's house, there was only the promise of another hit either by a hand (adult or mini) or a rolled newspaper. But there was one more complication that I need to share about this mess I found myself in.

I was pregnant.

Yes, just over a year old and pregnant. (Another good example of the lunacy of your dog-years-times-human-years equation. How many seven-year-olds do you know that would be expecting without its being a *National Enquirer* headline? Outside of Thailand, I mean.) And lucky me, it happened as a result of my first time, all orchestrated by my first human, who had now tacked "pimp" onto his resume.

I'd actually overheard the conversation, but was too naïve to give it a second thought. He was talking to a friend on the phone. "We should put Bitsy and Ralph together and sell the puppies," he'd said. Oh, I guess I better explain. This is pretty mortifying, but I need to tell you that my first human had named me "Bitsy."

Bitsy for Dog's sake. You name a Yorkie "Bitsy." You name a Toy Poodle "Bitsy." No canine over seven pounds should have to be called "Bitsy."

Bitsy. That was almost as bad as the beatings.

But I digress.

Well, I didn't give that overheard conversation a second thought until a few hours later. I'd been napping in the cardboard box that they'd passed off as my crate, when one of the minis ran into the room making a commotion. "Bitsy's got a boyfriend, Bitsy's got a boyfriend!" That's when my first human came into the room, picked me up with his calloused hands (and he was a bank teller, so Dog knows what he'd been up to), and carted me unceremoniously out into the backyard.

That's where I first saw him.

Ralph.

Ralph was—how shall I say? Ralph was as close to a human male as a canine could be. Broad shoulders. Dark. Strong. Panting and slobbering. Stupid too. Stupid stupid stupid. But I would learn about his character a little too late. My relationship with Ralph was a precursor to my continuing attraction to bad boys. I mean, why settle for a Dachshund when you can get a Rottweiler? Girls, I know you hear what I'm saying.

Ralph and I were together for about two minutes. There was sniffing there was a bit of playful biting, and then before I knew it, two paws on my back and he was gone. Not even a goodbye. I never saw Ralph again. As I said, just like a human male.

It didn't take long before I knew that I was with puppy. My hunger increased, I got tired at the drop of a chew toy. Unfortunately, the beatings from my human did not decrease. I'd already learned to do everything he and his minis said, but now if his orders weren't executed in record time, I'd get popped.

While my personality was never as frenetic as most of my breed, my impending maternity mellowed me even more. I found myself nesting, fluffing and rearranging the towels that lined my cardboard box, keeping myself just a bit cleaner than before. As I gained weight, it became harder to get comfortable, but I could feel that warm glow that most mothers speak of, and I loved it.

And I must confess, that as I drifted off to sleep, my thoughts would often turn to Ralph.

> *A dog is the only thing on Earth that loves you more than he loves himself.*
> Josh Billings

CHAPTER TWO

L-I-N-G-O AND LINGO WAS HIS NAME-O

I want to talk about language, yours and mine. Every canine is blessed with the ability to be at least bilingual. We're born, of course, with an intrinsic understanding of the canine tongue, but each of us comes to understand the language of our humans. As with humans, some are quicker to that understanding than others. It is sort of typical of the human arrogance that the depth of your willingness to learn canine linguistics ceases at body language.

"When the dog's head is dipped low to the floor," the expert begins, "and his hind quarters are elevated, the dog is telling you he wants to play."

How profound! Even the minis of your species know that. But I guess after all the hub-bub over immigration and making English an official language, I shouldn't be all that surprised about your continuing human-centricity. So I've decided to share with you some insights into the language of the canine world. I'm not, however, going to provide a Rosetta Stone. There are some things even humans need to earn, so until you put more effort into learning to speak Caninese, I'll keep it pretty basic.

Let's start with my name. As is your human custom, my mother named me at birth. Translated phonetically, my name is Gggrriff. That's akin to "Heather" in your world. And Gggrriff is my *real* name. Ruby is my slave name, as it were, an improvement on Bitsy to be sure, but artificially granted nonetheless. My name is also a clue as to why your species would have a tough time with the canine language; too many consonants for the human tongue to handle. Sort of like Slavic.

That said, your scientists are right about one thing for sure. We do a lot of communicating through smell.

While it's true that some of my lesser advanced canine brethren can be a bit, um, shall we say *intrusive* when it comes to their particular lack of finesse in nosing around a freshly met human (thankfully, I was bred correctly and can proudly state that I have not once violated a human nether region with my proboscis), most of us have you all figured out by the time you're within twenty feet. Here's what I was able to discern about my current human before we'd even made eye contact when we met for the first time:

1. He came straight from the gym, no shower.
2. He had a tuna salad sandwich for lunch on a sesame bagel, and a Pepsi—no, a Diet Pepsi.
3. There was no evidence of another human scent on him, so he was single, probably unlucky, and homely.
4. He had a new car.

Not bad, huh? Every unmarried woman out there (and more than a few men) wish they had that power. Would save a lot of morning-after embarrassment, right ? Talk about common scents.

Sorry, I have a weakness for puns.

Okay, so let's talk about marking territory. I mean, that's communication. Through the scent we leave behind us, we can tell the next canine coming along all the basics they need to know. "Gggriff was here, female, not interested in sex but wouldn't mind being friends (and as with humans, that basically tells a male to smell elsewhere), I share this block with a male Rotty and a female Lab."

And when we bark at one another? We're having a discussion, sometimes heated and territorial, sometimes protective of our humans, sometimes friendly. I can't go into any more detail. I told you earlier I won't reveal the language itself. So much has been taken from us, I must adhere to the canine code and not share what we're really saying in its entirety, our alphabet, etc. Let's just say that a lot of times, how you interpret us is not particularly accurate. Let me give you an example.

You know how you think it's cute to get us to bark on cue? "Speak! Speak!" you command, and very compliantly we sit, look up at you, and you hear "Bark! Bark!" Wanna know what we're really saying? Okay, it goes something like this.

Human: "Speak, Ruby! Speak!"

Ruby: "Asshole say 'Good girl.'"

Human: "Good girl, Ruby."

Then, you give us a cookie.

I need to tell you why you will not hear me refer to myself as a dog. For canines, using that term is blasphemous. Dog, in canine, is actually a reference to the Supreme Spirit Being. Where do you think, "In Dog We Trust" came from? We canines believe that in the beginning, Dog created the Earth, and having constructed the ultimate playground, followed that up by creating the first canines, male and female. Canine religion splits up into various sects at this point, belief systems varying as to whether or not that first pair were Labradors, Dalmatians, Beagles, or Great Danes. While, as is the case with our language, I am somewhat averse to sharing much of the sacred word with you, in giving you a glimpse into our spirituality, let me share with you some of the prophecy contained in our Holy Book, *Dog for Dummies*.

"And Dog so loved the world he vowed one day to send a representative worthy of his wisdom and beneficence to the Earth in human form, to share his grace with thee. It is up to each canine (and the humans who serve them), to be aware and on watch, to welcome this holiest of holy prophets into their homes. She will be born into poverty in the south of a great and vast country, and will journey through great metropolosi, all the while gathering followers, pounds, and hairstyles. Be not put off by her changing shape, instead be aware of her message, for some day, she will be embraced by the multitudes. Be not distracted by false idols; for many will come offering pretense and facade. Some will wear annoying glasses, others espousing contentious confrontation.

"But the true prophet will be known by her works. For she will command humans to read and give them cars. She will appear to them each weekday afternoon for sixty minutes, (check local times for repeats).

"She will love canines as her own. And she will earn more money than Dog.

"Her human name will be a derivative of the human interpretation of our language. The human ear will hear us say "Bow Wow" as we worship the one true Dog and await his holy daughter. But know this; we will be praying for the emergence of that daughter and the fulfillment of prophecy. Yes, they will hear us saying, "Bow Wow," but we will actually be chanting ow-ow ... o w o w O W O W Op Wi Opr Win ..."

Canine sects are contentious about various points of theology, but they do agree on two things; Dog is fallible (proven by his decision to create humans as canine playmates, that experiment, of course, an unmitigated disaster), and there is only one intermediary between Dog and his faithful.

That, naturally, would be St. Bernard.

If you must label me, I'm a beagle mix, yes, but first and foremost I consider myself to be a Canine-American. I was born here just like you, and while I enjoy considerably fewer obvious freedoms than humans (although notably, we are free from being taxed, jury duty and spending time with in-laws), I am grateful not to be Canine-English (where dog food is a half-step up from human cooking), Canine-Korean (where I would *be* a meal), or Canine-Arabic (*We're* filthy animals? Have you ever had a whiff of one of those outdoor bazaars?). Despite the challenges of being a Canine-American, I love my country. I'm a respectful patriot. And unlike Dick Cheney, I would never pee on the Constitution.

On the subject of labels, I should talk a bit about the human names you deign to bestow on us. It does seem like you take a certain perverse pleasure in that power. Myself, I don't much care for the cutesy-poo names. I'm already on record about "Bitsy." Since I'm sort of speaking for the entire species here, let me suggest that these names are over. That is, please don't use the following any more:

1. *Spot.* That would be like you naming one of your minis "Pimple."
2. *Rover.* Begs for a self-fulfilling fate of life on the lam.
3. *Precious.* That name jumped the shark after *Silence of the Lambs.*
4. *Cujo.* Stephen King should be sued for libel.
5. *Lady.* Lady is a title, not a name.
6. *Queenie.* Same as above, unless the canine is male and into Clay Aiken.
7. *Rex.* Mundane. False bravado. T-Rex is acceptable, has a little more flair.
8. *The Regent Jordan of St. Anselm Field or any such over-long show-dog name.* I hesitate to add this, because these names do serve a purpose. They tell you that the human who bestowed the title is maladjusted, likely beyond hope, and should be lobotomized before he ends up in a clock tower with a semi-automatic.
9. *Fido.* Fido comes from the Latin, roughly interpreted as "my nimrod of an owner has zero sense of originality."
10. *Spike.* You spike a football. You spike a drink while watching football. Your blood pressure spikes because you bet on football. But you do not name a canine Spike.
11. *Odie.* The cat got top billing in the lame comic strip. Nuff said.
12. *Prince.* A diminutive musician, not a canine.

And as long as we're wrapping up the subject of labels, please remember that I am more than a Canine-American, I'm a female canine. I am *not* a bitch. Do not call me that.

Ann Coulter, on the other hand ...

🐾 🐾 🐾

My human is amazed by my intelligence. Little did he know. Anyway, here are the words and phrases he thought comprised my ability to understand the human language:

Sit. Stay. Lie down. Breakfast. Dinner. Bacon. Wanna go for a ride?

Walkies. Short walkies. Long walkies. Jump. Go seepies. Go potty.

Do your duty. Cross (as in, "Cross the street.") Bunny. Kelly (My human's for-all-intents-and-purposes-adopted son.) Mandy (Kelly's wife) Dakota (Kelly's dog) Wanna go outside? Island. (The little patch of grass at the end of the cul-de-sac that I use as a bathroom.) Cuddle.

Gimme paw. Gimme kisses. Kathy (The sitter.)

While we're on the subject of vocabulary, here are some of the pet names (no pun intended) that my current human calls me, usually when we are out on a walkie.

Ruby, Boo Bear, Poo Bear, Fur Butt, Tubby Girl, Fatso Girl, Monkey, Monkey Butt, Ruby Doo, Ru Ru, Fur Monkey, Ru-Bu-Cop, Chunker, Chunky Girl, Chunk Monster, Love Bunny, Bunny Butt, Munchkin, Fur Ball, Happy Girl, Stubborn, Pretty Girl, Pertty Baby. Kissy Dog, Baby Dog, Sweetie Butt, Goofus, Goofus Girl. Ru Ru Nuts. Ru Ru Nitsa.

I have plenty of reason to hate him.

The more I see of men, the more I admire dogs.
Jeanne Marie Roland

CHAPTER THREE

THE GREAT ESCAPE

I was alone when my babies arrived. Britney Spears was readier for motherhood than I was. You see, I could not rely on any maternal advice or direction. I had been snatched away from my own mother when I was eight weeks old, never to see her again.

What I remember of Mama was wonderful. She was a beautiful girl, little more than a puppy herself when she gave birth to my sisters, brothers and me. She kept us fed and warm, refereed our playful tussles, and held us in line any time her humans were around. I look quite a lot like her, although I got my father's shorter ears and tail. Papa always seemed a bit distracted, but he would play with us when we were in the mood, and every so often he would gently clean our ears.

I recall my childhood, brief as it was, as happy. My siblings and I had the obligatory fights over food and teat position, you know, just like you humans. We had a huge yard, green as far as the nose could smell.

When we were inside the house, we were only allowed in the kitchen area of Mama and Papa's humans.

(We did manage one surreptitious foray into the den; surreptitious, that is, until my younger brother opted to make a snack of a wire connected to Mama's human's computer. Suffice to say, it got ugly.) The floor was slippery, and we eagerly snapped up any scraps that the humans, sometimes purposely, dropped.

Mama's humans were very kind, as I recall, and I never remember Mama complaining about them at all.

Until that fateful day.

It was a Tuesday, and the day had started like any other. We had just begun eating the food that Mama's human had been leaving out for us in these adorable little blue bowls. Suddenly, Mama's male human reached down for me like he'd done many times before. I suspected nothing more than to get a playful kiss.

But this time would be different. After scooping me up, he was oddly cold as he toted me out into the back yard. There, a human male I had never seen before, with his own two minis, was waiting. Mama's human put me down, and I started running around, sniffing the plants, playing with the two minis. Being me, simple as that.

"She's yours if you want her," said Mama's human.

And just like that, I was gone, carried against my will into a car by this strange human male. I was squealing for my Mama, nipping and clawing at the minis who were trying to keep a tight grip around my torso. They covered me with human kisses, rubbed my back and belly. But that kind treatment wasn't enough to prevent me from being terrified. I kept trying to tear my way to the window. I wanted my Mama, I wanted to see my brothers and sisters. But it was not to be. It wasn't five minutes before one of the minis screeched to the adult human who was driving. "I wanna name her Bitsy."

"Sounds like a fine name to me," the human behind the steering wheel said. And the mini looked at me, grabbed my cheeks, shook my head side to side and said, "You're my little Bitsy from now on. You're my cutest little Bitsy. Oh Daddy,

I love my Bitsy! Bitsy, Bitsy, Bitsy. Do you like your new name?"

I puked.

🐾 🐾 🐾

The first impression I got from viewing my new home would prove to be accurate. I remember hearing the crackling scrunch of tires against gravel, as the car pulled into a driveway that was shaped like a broad "S."

No sooner had we stopped than the mini who I hadn't puked on grabbed me and made for the backyard. He peeled open a chain link gate and dropped me onto a patch of well-worn, brownish stubble that might have been grass in a former life.

"Come on Bitsy. Let's play!" said the mini. Instead, I froze in my tracks. There were three bicycles in various states of disrepair strewn about the yard, which was bordered by an enormous white-washed wooden fence. A rotting maroon picnic table sat lopsidedly on a cracked cement porch, just in front of a sliding glass door that had never experienced the benefits of Windex. The outer walls of the house were made of aluminum siding that, at one time, might have been white.

The adult human opened the sliding door and peered back at his two minis, who were trying to coax me to play. "And remember, the first time that thing 'goes' in the house, I'm beating the tar out of you."

His words weren't exactly Lincolnesque, but the minis took them to heart. They made it their mission to teach me good bathroom habits, and in so doing adhered to, shall we say, "Old School" tactics. Look, its embarrassing to write about these things, but I was just a couple of months old. Accidents were going to happen, and frankly I didn't know at the time that it was an accident to go whenever or wherever nature called. So I simply went, and they simply hit me when I did.

"Bad Bitsy!" Thwack.

Then came the "training" routine because, apparently, they were convinced that pain wasn't a good enough negative reinforcement. No, why just inflict pain alone when humiliation is such an attractive side dish!

So the thwack was swiftly followed by one of the minis shoving my nose into whatever bodily fluid I happened to have left behind, followed by another thwack, and then a grab of the collar. The sliding door would open, and I'd be tossed outside. After a few days of this, I was just thankful they remembered to open the sliding door.

The leash training I got was similarly barbaric. It consisted of the adult tethering a lead to my collar, and dragging me around the back yard until my little paws could match his speed. And if I fell too far behind or was distracted by a tasty smell?

Thwack. "Keep up Bitsy."

Thwack. "Bitsy! I said heel."

Thwack. "That one was because I could."

I'm not going to lie, the thwacks hurt. But Bitsy? My Mama did not give me that name, and no matter what slave name they were going to put on me, no amount of thwacking was going to get me to buy into "Bitsy."

Or so I told myself at the time.

Even typing that accursed name makes me want to barf.

That comfy-looking couch that faced the TV? I hopped up on there once … just once … to cuddle and nestle. "Not on the furniture, Bitsy, bad girl!" Thwack. It wasn't long before the beatings took their effect. "Sit Bitsy." And I did. "Lie down Bitsy." Whatever you say. "Heel Bitsy." Yes Massuh.

My name be Bitsy. Sing with me everybody, "Swing low, sweet chariot …"

🐾   🐾   🐾

It got so bad, that by the time I was eight months old, any time a new person came into the house, my automatic reaction was to flinch. Friends of the minis would come by and remark how cute I was, but by the time they took their first and totally unthreatening step towards me, I would tear off and hide under the nearest piece of furniture. (Unthreatening though they might have been, they were sickening nonetheless. I mean the baby talk. "Ooooh. Wook at duh perrty baby. Come heeer my dittle girl." Like nails on a chalk board. When you boil it all down, you humans are really a strange lot.)

Oh, and I don't want to forget about the fireworks. I have no idea how long I was at this wretched place when I got to experience my first Fourth of July celebration. My human and his minis had a bunch of people over. I loved the smells of the burgers, hot dogs and the like. The day had started with so much promise. I was sure to get a lot of tasty morsels from plate spillage. Any canine worth his or her salt can count on a certain level of human clumsiness to bring us joy. Add some alcohol to the mix and I was sure I was going to eat more than a Roman Emperor at a pre-orgy feast.

I spent most of the day off in a corner. The visiting humans tried to be nice, but I was still gun-shy, still not very trusting.

When a bit of hamburger bun dropped off a table, I'd dash out from under one of the chairs, grab the sublime treat, and beat a hasty retreat. This system proved profitable and satisfying until dusk.

When it began to get dark, the minis began pestering their father. Then I saw some of the other adult humans, all of whom were Budweisered to the gills by this point, join in the discussion. My human heaved a deep sigh, vanished into the house for a minute, and then returned with some sort of package in his hand that prompted the minis to jump up and down in a spasm of joy that made me think trouble was ahead.

I didn't see what happened next, but I heard it.

BANG.

BANG. BANG. BANG.

Fireworks.

Now for those of you who don't know, dogs have a heightened sense of hearing. Loud noises (and any notes uttered by Celine Dion or Mariah Carey) are basically intolerably painful. So these sudden explosive bursts sent a lightning bolt directly into my skull. It would get worse.

"Hey," said one of the minis. "I know how we can get Bitsy out from under her chair."

Yes, dear readers, it's true. With full approval of the adult human, one of the minis lit one of those firecrackers and rolled it under the chair that was providing my safe haven.

I do not have the literary skills to accurately describe the abject terror, combined with mind-numbing pain that I felt. I bolted from my safe place, and all that did was encourage the minis to chase after me. One, then another of the missiles were sent in my direction. I tore from one side of the yard to the other, unable to find any place out of their diabolical reach. I don't know how long the assault lasted, but I'm sure it only ended because their supply had been exhausted.

I spent the rest of the night sleepless, shivering in fear, missing Mama more than ever. If there was a hell, this was it.

I'd been a few weeks along in my pregnancy, and was glowing. I was still thinking that Ralph, my sweet prince of a dog, would come back to rescue me from this white trash nightmare I was living in. But day after long day, made more painful because my pregnancy forced me into the odd accident or two in the house (which were each met with the anticipated slap and a renewed round of nose-in-the-piss), it became clear that I was in this alone. If there was one thing I knew for sure, it was that I did not want my babies brought into the world in this atmosphere of violence. So each day, when my human let me out into the yard, I waddled around for a bit and lay down, feigning sleep until he either went back into the house or passed out in his torn up lawn chair, cigarette dangling from his lips, ashes falling gently onto the top of his can of Blatz. Then, I would quietly walk over to that little area by the fence where the dirt had moved so easily and continue my dig. Each day, I would make a bit more headway; each day I told myself, I was closer to whatever was beyond that hideous fence. I was ready to experience my own personal *Shawshank Redemption*.

I told you I watch a lot of TNT.

❖ ❖ ❖

The right time finally arrived. My human came home from work almost every day for lunch, made a beeline for the sliding door and let me into the yard. He would spend thirty minutes every day eating and then slipping off to the couch for a cat-nap (more about "cat" terms later). You humans are such creatures of habit. The minis were at school, the neighborhood was quiet. I'd had the dirt around my escape route loosened as much as possible without anyone noticing. My window of opportunity was narrowing. I was getting so big that I could feel my babies beginning to kick, and if I'd waited any longer I risked having them born into this dreadful house, not to mention if I'd gotten any bigger, I wouldn't have been able to dig deep enough for me to get out.

So at noon, like every weekday, I heard the front door open. I went to give him a cursory greeting, a begrudged wag of the tail. He grunted without making eye contact, walked to the sliding door, and out I went. I looked back, and as soon as I saw him swing open the refrigerator door, I made my way to the patch of dirt and clawed at it. I had about seven minutes of dig time before he'd hit the sofa for his nap. I had almost all the dirt removed when I heard him push his chair away from the table. Just a few minutes now …

"Bitsy. Bitsy."

Damn. He was calling me. And there was this gaping hole in the ground, totally exposed, no time to cover it back up. He would be sure to see it. As soon as I heard the first screech of the rusty screen door, I simply plopped my ample body on top of the hole, feigning sleep.

"Oh, you lazy mutt." The door squeaked again, and his footsteps trailed off towards the den.

Too close, but there was no time to worry. I quickly ducked low, squeezed my head through the opening, and forced my now-Rubenesque figure beneath the bottom of the wooden fence. A searing bolt of pain shot through me as I caught my ear on a splinter (the scar is still there), but I dared not yelp. "Push," I told myself. "Push harder." My first two legs pulled, and pulled harder, my stomach dragging through the mercifully soft dirt. I leveraged my back legs, and gave a strong kick, and then tumbled forward.

I'd made it to the other side.

The triumph I felt at that very second was dizzying, but I knew I was not safe. So, overweight, filthy and bleeding, I broke into a hellacious sprint. My desire for freedom prevented me from taking in these new and foreign surroundings. The only destination I had was "far away." After what seemed like hours, I found myself in a wooded area. I could hear the sounds of cars in the distance, but all I could see were trees and grass. The air was filled with the wondrous smells of the wild. As night fell, I was chilled, to be sure, but I burrowed into some leaves, curled up, and slept a blessedly dreamless sleep.

I woke up the next morning refreshed, but racked with hunger pangs. Grass would be my diet that morning, and while I craved some good squirrel, those manipulatively and deceptively cute rodents were tough to catch when I was at my fighting weight, forget about being as pregnant as I was.

I was now the size of a small bungalow, my nipples virtually dragging on the ground every time I took a step. Pregnancy had done to me what gravity is sure to do to Pamela Anderson in short order.

But now there would be one more challenge to deal with. I didn't need any motherly guidance to let me know what was happening. The searing pain literally forced me onto my side. I wanted desperately to scream out, but my overriding fear of being found by my human stifled that natural need. Within moments, the pain gave way to indescribable bliss as I heard the first little whiney whelp, followed shortly by another, then another, then another, then one more. And before I knew it, I was accosted by five furry little mouths pushing and shoving, jostling for position to have their first meal. The emotions I was experiencing were myriad and contradictory. Joy to the point of tears, fear to the point of panic. I'd escaped just in time, but had my instinct to protect my babies left us all vulnerable to whatever the wilds of Indiana held?

My little old dog, a heartbeat at my feet.
Edith Wharton

CHAPTER FOUR

TRAINING DAY

This is a subject I approach with much ambivalence. First, to acknowledge canine trainers at all strikes me as being a little like admitting that we can't raise our own. I hasten to point out that canines did fine, thank you very much, in the wilds for eons long before we were "domesticated" (read: enslaved). So for sanity's sake, let's view dog training as similar to the educational system you trust your minis to. There are hundreds of theories about proper human education, and all of them are successful to some degree or another. Montessori schools have produced many an Ivy League standout, but inner city schools with overcrowded classrooms boast some of the most dedicated and able (and underpaid) teachers in the world.

For a time, corporal punishment was not only accepted, it was de rigueur, especially when applied by nineteenth-century schoolmarms or twentieth-century nuns. (Not that there is no way to easily distinguish the difference between those two in matters of dress, temperament or romantic attachments.) For a time, learning by rote was the prevailing thought, and by the 1960s you were experimenting with open classrooms, relaxed dress codes, and heightened in-class participation.

Despite the different approaches, they all had one end result. No one could justify algebra for use in the real world.

Canine training evolved similarly. Humans have progressed from accepting brute force and rubbing our noses in feces, to clickers and "natural dog training." For every training "expert" who espouses using treats as rewards in the training process, you can find another who thinks it's a poor method that should be replaced by having your canine perform a task simply because he or she should want to, the sole motivation being to please the "master."

As if.

That latter theory can be illustrated in this oft-repeated human conversation:

Husband: "Do you want me to do the dishes?"
Wife: "No."
Husband: "Okay, I'm going to watch the game."
Wife: Sobs.
Husband: "What's wrong?"
Wife: "You're not going to do the dishes!"
Husband: "You said you didn't want me to..."
Wife: "I don't want you to do the dishes, I want you to *want* to do the dishes."

In the real world, a spouse who wants to motivate her other half to perform a task she needs him to complete takes this approach:

Husband: "Do you want me to do the dishes?"
Wife: "Only if you want to have sex tonight."
Result: Sparkling dishes.

If you can't tell, I am a proponent of the treat approach to training. I am motivated principally by what I want to do. Unfailingly, what I want to do is have a cookie. I'll compromise at times of course, but I want that cookie. You have the cookie, I do not. How do I get the cookie? You want me to sit in order for me to get the cookie, I'll sit till the cows come home. I am not going to sit simply because you want me to sit.

While we're on the subject, why in the hell do you guys want to see us sit so much in the first place? What exactly do you find so Dog damn amusing about seeing us execute the simple act of sitting down?

You're not the ones getting the blasted cookie!

From where I "sit," it boils down to this: power, that weird human compunction to lord it over another breathing creature, human or otherwise.

Power corrupts, absolute power while dangling a cookie corrupts absolutely.

Clicker training is a scream. Know why we respond so well to it? Because we know the sound annoys the crap out of you. Click away people, no problem here.

Then there's the matter of shock collars. These sadistic little goodies are still used in some quarters today, but thankfully they are going the way of the electric chair. (Except in Texas, where I think they are still very popular. The shock collar, not the electric chair. I can see where you might have been confused. And while we're on the subject, if the death penalty is such a deterrent, how come the need for so many executions in Texas? Just asking.) Which, of course, is as it should be. Wonder who first thought of using shock treatment as a way to elicit positive behavior? My guess was it was either a psychologist from the 1940s, or a W. Bush administration lawyer from the first term.

Or the second term.

As I write this, one of the most popular items on the canine-related market is the Invisible Fence. This is much different, of course, than the shock collar. The shock collar produces pain when the canine *does* something unacceptable. The Invisible Fence produces pain when the canine *goes* somewhere unacceptable.

So you see, it's a whole different deal. "Does" starts with a *d,* "goes" starts with a *g.* Totally different.

There are other training approaches and thoughts, of course, and here are a few that I'll summarize with excerpted direct quotes, followed by my insightful commentary.

OBEDIENCE THEORY: "Involves a moral judgment in that the dog is good or bad ... training follows a pattern of increasing the amount of force in stages if the preceding one fails."

For you history buffs, this is the same school of thought that gave you The Inquisition.

REINFORCEMENT THEORY: "Behavior reinforced positively will be repeated."

This school of thought produced the "Me" Generation.

COGNITIVE THEORY: "Desired responses (by the dog) will bring reward, praise, play, food from the handler, while undesired behaviors all bring undesired responses from the handler; either ignoring the dog, no attention, no fun, *maybe even a little unpleasantness."*

Maybe even a little unpleasantness? How sinister does that sound. Read the Cognitive Theory out loud in a German accent and tell me you don't get totally creeped out.

🐾   🐾   🐾

There are tons of people out there who've made quite a name (and quite a fortune) for themselves training canines. I'm going to focus on a couple of them.

Barbara Woodhouse: The Woman Who Coined The Term "Walkies."

This is the elderly English woman who published the best seller, *No Bad Dogs*. Most of us four-leggers embraced this brave lady's message that "there is no such thing as a bad dog … there are only inexperienced owners." Yes, she had bad teeth, yes she wore those unbearably sensible shoes, and yes, she had the worst case of "cankles" known to modern man. But what she said was more important than how she looked.

I give her huge props for changing the way most people saw us, for showing that working with us in a more compassionate manner would yield superior results. While a lot of my canine contemporaries are still bitter about the previous medieval methods humans used on us, I am more forgiving. We do well to remember that you used to look at training your own minis much the same way you trained us; by delicately balancing just the right level of physical violence. You know, enough to evoke fear, but not so much that the raised welts were visible to schoolteachers.

Here's what Ms. Woodhouse said about working with canines:

"You need hands that on touching a dog, send messages of love and sympathy to its brain … a voice with a wide range of tones to convey orally your wishes … You need eyes that tell the dog who watches them what you are feeling. Above all, you need telepathy, so that the dog thinks with you."

I know what you're thinking. "Telepathy?" Admittedly, this may be a tad too New Ageish, and thankfully that portion of her message wasn't widely publicized before her book became a huge seller or she got her TV show. But she was to canines as Dr. Spock was to children of the 60s.

And look how well that worked out.

$$\text{\raisebox{0pt}{🐾}} \quad \text{🐾} \quad \text{🐾}$$

Cesar Millan: The Dog Whisperer

This guy has his own TV show, just like everyone else who has impressed Miss Oprah at one time or another. I do not deny that he has done some good things, but I am left with the nagging impression that he is little more than a short, Hispanic, hairier version of Dr. Phil. They're certainly alike in the area of sensitivity to those who come to them for help.

Harried Housewife: "Dr. Phil, my husband is cheating on me, my kids don't respect my home's rules, and my parents call me a failure."

Dr. Phil: "That's because you never met a doughnut you could say 'no' to and you dress off the rack at Wal-Mart. Where's your self esteem?"

Cesar's philosophy springs from the canine pack mentality (if you're looking for a human correlation, think "birth order") found in nature, our familial order when we are left to our own devices. The key, he posits, to effective training is to make sure that the human is the leader of the pack in every household.

Smart. Learning from nature. What better way to learn can their possibly be than from learning what nature has to teach?

Whenever you see Mr. Millan in a promotional video, he is usually surrounded by dogs numbering in the double digits, of all breeds and temperaments, all submissive to Mr. Millan because he has established himself as the Alpha Dog. A key part of establishing his position is this noise he makes that I can't adequately describe on paper. Well, here, let me quote from his web site:

"At appearances throughout the country, Cesar draws sellout crowds of fans and dogs ready to hear Cesar's signature "Tsst!"

Tsst.

I kid you not.

Tsst. Not a vowel in the neighborhood.

I'm a canine. I know lots of canines. We talk. Never, not once, not ever, have I heard another canine say to me, "Hey, doesn't that 'Tsst' just send you?"

There's something else going on here folks. Something dark, something creepy. Hypnosis of some sort, or maybe it's the telepathy thing Barbara Woodhouse was talking about. My theory is that "Tsst" is the key hypnotic word. You know how hypnotists create the suggestion in their subjects that any time they hear the word "Chicken" they'll automatically flap their arms and cluck? Same principle. Want another sign that I'm on to something? Do you know what Cesar's wife's name is?

Illusion. No shit.

There is one compelling reason to keep watching his show. One day—and this is sure to happen—one day he's going to slip up. One day, when he's old and his dentures aren't secure enough, "Tsst" will come out "Tfffwwwt." He'll use that stern voice and that commanding body language, but the pack will sense weakness. Just a crack maybe, but weakness just the same.

His pack will begin to move closer to him, surround him. He'll "Tfffwwwt," then "Tfffwwwt" again. The fear of realization will envelop him. He'll know that he's doomed when he sees visions of all of those wonderfully spirited canines whose wills he's broken over the years rushing at him.

And just as he learned from nature, we canines also have learned first-hand from nature. When the leader of the pack becomes too weak to lead, the strong survive.

Now that will be compelling television.

Tsst indeed.

With the help of his canine pack, Mr. Millan will have gone full circle from "Dog Whisperer" to "Ghost Whisperer."

Dogs' lives are too short, their only fault, really.
Carlotta Monterrey O'Neill

CHAPTER FIVE

RESCUE ME

So there I was, splayed like a beached whale, lying in the middle of a forest with five mouths to feed. My recollection is foggy, but I believe I was there for two or three days, my babies crying, me keeping them warm against the cool evening breeze. I was in no shape to go off and hunt for food for myself, and while the babies were feeding, they were sapping what little energy I had left.

I went in and out of consciousness on that third day, but as weak as I was, I was still able to sense a nearing presence. My sense of smell was still strong, and I knew it was a human. I wanted to gather my children and flee, but it would have been no use. If it was my human who had found us, I was resigned to the fact that we would be returned to the house, and I would be beaten. But at least we'd be able to eat. The smell of this human was different though, more welcoming, safer.

This human was a stranger. He was tall, and I remember a strong glint of light reflecting off whatever it was he was wearing on his chest. He was dressed in some sort of brown uniform from head to toe. He approached us slowly, almost gently despite his seemingly unnatural size. He was bigger than my human, much bigger, and almost square. The nearer he came, the darker it got, his massive shoulders shielding the sun behind him. He was within inches now, and I recoiled naturally as I did with all humans, at the same time turning my back to him as a way of protecting my babies.

"No, it's okay little girl. No one's going to hurt your babies."

I heard the words, but even as weak as I was, I wasn't going to believe them. For all I knew, our lives may have been at stake.

"It's all going to be okay," he cooed. Then, I felt the brush of his enormous fingers against my spine. I cringed, but he kept stroking me, gently. He moved his fingers to the back of my neck. I was so tired. No food, no water, feeding my babies. He kept caressing my neck, and I fell into a dead sleep.

I was awakened from my desperate sleep by a bouncing jolt. We were in a car, that I knew instantly. My children and I lay on a thick blanket on the floor of a back seat. I looked up and saw some sort of fence or barrier that extended up from the top of the seat, and the stranger I assumed was driving because I could hear him having a discussion with a disembodied voice that seemed to crackle from the front part of the car. But there were no other humans in the car.

"She looks like a beagle, I think. Five puppies. Yeah, I'm going to take her to the shelter."

The shelter? I had no idea what that was. The only saving grace of the utter lack of control I had of the situation was this one truth: where there were humans, there was food, and at that moment I knew I would readily trade my freedom for a single slice of bacon. We were in the car for only a short time before it came to a stop. The human got out of the car, and after a few minutes, I could sense that he was with two others.

All three faces peered into the car, their noses crushed and contorted against the window (Dog, you humans can be funny looking). I couldn't make out what they were saying.

Soon, the door opposite from where I was huddled swung open. The tall man in the brown uniform was standing behind two female humans, both attired in flower-print smocks with hospital-issue pea-green cotton pants. The first one through the door wore Dog-awful glasses circa 1971, and had the smell of dozens of canines all over her. She had a kind face though, weathered, very Shar-Pei, and she moved towards me slowly, talking calmly, obviously trying to earn my trust.

"Oh, look at this nice new Mommy we have here. And the mommy has such pretty babies."

(Question: Why in the hell do you humans feel the urge to talk human-baby talk every time you see one of us? I mean, let's examine the logic. Do you think the human language is easier for canines to understand if you talk like an imbecile? Okay, back to the story.)

Yes, this mommy has nice pretty babies and you better keep your distance or this mommy is going to sink her teeth into your plump little palm and you have no idea if I've ever had rabies shots.

"Now, you pretty girl. You be a good girl and we're going to give you some good treats, and make a nice home for you and your babies."

Treats? Did I hear treats?

She inched closer. I pulled back my jowls to show my teeth, but that simple act exhausted me. I was going to lose this war.

"No pretty girl. You don't have to bite me. I'll be very nice to you and your babies." And with that, she began to pet my forehead. I pulled back and averted my eyes from her.

"Someone hit you real bad once, didn't they," she said.

If it had only been once. I hope you didn't have to graduate from college to make that diagnosis, Miss Marple.

With a deftness I did not think her capable of, in an instant she had her hands under the blanket, and had scooped my kids and me up in one motion, pivoted out of the car, and began a hurried pace back towards a brick building with a green awning. The other female human had the front door open, and the tall man trailed behind us. Once inside, we were placed inside what can only be called a pen. The walls weren't very high, the floor was very much like the kitchen floor at Mama's human's home. Slippery, cool, comfortable and familiar.

"Thanks officer," said one female. "We'll keep them until the pups are weaned, then put them up for adoption."

Whoa!

"Do you adopt out most of your strays?"

"We're about 75 percent. We'll keep the adult four weeks after we put them up, and if no one takes her, well …"

Well? Well what?

"So you're not a no-kill."

"No. We just get too many. But she's a cute dog. Someone will want her."

It did not take long for me to settle into the new routine. This "shelter" place was spotless. Any time any one of my babies made a mess, it seemed like only seconds before one of the pleasant (if somewhat dim-witted) helpers was there to clean things up. The staff was very respectful of my babies, and they'd obviously had experience dealing with situations like mine. Even still, their care did little to alleviate my fear of humans, and I continued to recoil every time they came near. But very quickly, their food and water regimen took hold, and I began feeling a lot more like my old self. The panic and discombobulation of my escape and all that it entailed had passed now, and with the ensuing clarity came the realization that I had yet to name my precious brood.

I gave this task a lot of thought. Names are important, and I wanted my kids to have the names I gave them as a reminder of our bond. See, I was still not savvy enough to understand that it was customary after eight or nine weeks passed to have our canine babies separated from us by humans, and sold off for profit. (And if this practice doesn't scream for a Constitutional amendment, Defense of Marriage Act be damned, nothing does.) I didn't know that what happened to me is something every Mama canine faced. I didn't know that in just a few short weeks, I would be facing the very same thing.

The names I settled on were equivalent to your Matthew, Marcus, Lucas, Jonah, and Angela. It was amazing how quickly they all formed their own little personalities, and equally amazing how different every one of them looked. Lucas, Jonah, and Angela definitely favored me. The beagle gene carried heavily with them. But Matthew and Marcus? Every time I looked at those precious faces, I was reminded of my one and only love. Ralph.

As kind as the humans who ran the shelter were, and as solid and functional as the accommodations were, I was never able to get used to the lack of privacy. Unlike in my first human's house, if I wanted to go to the bathroom, I had to be accompanied by a shelter drone. I mean, it was mortifying to have to do my business under constant watch. At my first home, I had the yard and the type of privacy a real lady should expect. As the weeks passed, that never got any better. It wasn't just the staff of the place; they had a job to do and I understood that. But the longer our stay, the more strange humans came around, poking their fingers into our cage, cooing that abominable baby talk. The staff that accompanied these voyeurs were, in my mind, nothing but enablers.

"A state trooper found the female with the puppies who were just days old. They're about five weeks along now, and we'll look at adopting them out in another several weeks."

With that, I knew what the real price of my lost freedom was to be. As had happened with me, I was going to be separated from my kids. A matter of weeks? The thought of another escape crossed my mind, but I knew it would be no good. This place was buttoned down tighter than an Amish bridesmaid. There was nowhere to dig, nowhere to run.

It was not my nature to accept defeat, no matter how demure and afraid I looked to humans. But this time was different. So I made up my mind to focus all my energies on lavishing every single bit of attention I had on my babies. I wanted them to remember me like I remembered Mama.

When the day arrived that I had long dreaded, I was as ready as I could be. The shelter staff separated my kids from me slowly. They'd take one or two at a time, first for several minutes, then for hours. But they always brought them back to me before lights-out. The traffic at my kennel door had begun to increase.

More strangers were stopping by. The frequency with which the staff would take one of my babies off with them and return them some time later picked up.

Jonah was the first not to come back.

This particular stranger had stopped by three times already. That third time turned out to be strike three, and as soon as he showed up that last time, I knew. As the staff member fiddled with the kennel door, I ran over towards Jonah, licked his adorable white and brown face, and whispered, "Mama will never forget you."

The most playful and trusting of my kids, Jonah looked at me with an innocence that tore my heart apart, yipped as if he was off on just another routine play date, and was gone. I ambled back over to my blanket and lay down. I needed to stay strong for my other four, and as I turned my face from them to hide my expression of grief, I was suddenly accosted from all sides by four hopping sets of paws, tongues, and noses, all hell-bent on making me laugh.

Thankfully, they succeeded.

Oddly enough, that was the very moment I stopped feeling sad about my memories of Mama. At that very moment, I simply treasured the fact that I had a great Mama, that I'd given birth to a great Jonah. The joy of my time with them suddenly outweighed the pain of losing them.

And that, dear readers, is what real freedom is.

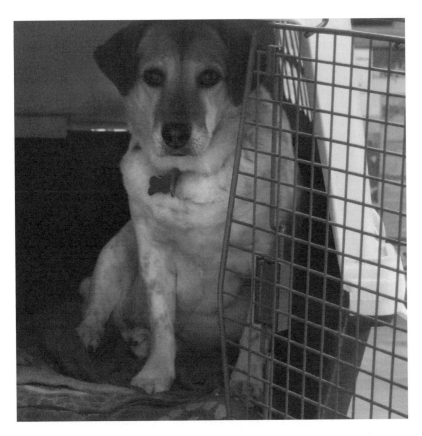

America is a large friendly dog in a very small room. Every time it wags it's tail, it knocks down a chair.

Arnold Toynbee

CHAPTER SIX

RUBY'S TIPS FOR BETTER LIVING

PART 1: DIET AND EXCERCISE

I'm home a lot, so I watch a lot of TV and listen to a lot of radio. So I thought I'd take a chapter here and give you some advice on topics you humans seem to obsess over. Let's start with diet.

As you're aware, during my pregnancy I had my own battle of the bulge. But in researching for this chapter, and wanting to make sure the advice I gave you came from more than my own personal experience, I did a Google search for a sample of human diet plans. There were 23,500,000 options. No joke, look it up. As a service to you, I'll break down what I found into easy-to-understand categories.

᛭   ᛭   ᛭

1. Food-specific diets: (These are real, honest-to-goodness, legitimate diets that you humans have bought into.)

Sugar Buster Diet (Sounds violent, doesn't it?); Grapefruit Diet (the brainchild of farmers in Texas and Florida, no doubt); Apple Cider Vinegar Diet (Sounds more like a new-age douche to me.); Fiber Diet (or "Look out, below!"); Ice Cream Diet (adhered to by most humans, as far as I can tell); Fruit Diet (more all-inclusive than the Grapefruit Diet); Vinegar Diet (Now we're back to old-school douche.); Cabbage Soup Diet (the secret behind all those svelte Slavic washerwomen); Low Salt Diet (You eat less and taste less.); Wheat-free Diet (because wheat is so fattening); Peanut Butter Diet (After a few days, you can't open your mouth anymore, hence the ensuing calorie loss.); Gluten-Free Diet (I still can't tell you exactly what gluten really is, but it sounds gross.); Lemonade Diet (which leaves your mouth in a deformed pucker, thereby limiting calorie intake); Rice Diet (or "Condoleeza's Secret"); Water Diet (Wonder why this works?); and the Low Potassium Diet (because nothing says weight loss like having leg cramps).

2. Diets Named After Human Beings: (Again, all real diets.)

Ann Fletcher's Thin For Life (Sounds more like a playground taunt to me.); Dr. Andrew Weil Diet (caloric reduction because everything that enters your mouth goes through a hairy strainer); Dr. Dean Ornish Diet (His motto is "Eat More, Weigh Less." Unfortunately the "more" are the foods you already don't like.); Dr. Phil's Ultimate Weight Solution (a little too Third-Reichish for my taste, as is Dr. Phil); Jenny Craig (I think Kirstie Alley's a scream, so I'll let this one go.); Perricone Diet (His anti-wrinkle diet is reviled in the Shar-Pei community.); The Pritikin Principle (Sounds like a Robert Ludlum thriller.); Scarsdale Diet (Get someone to shoot you; the weight will fly off.); and the Suzanne Sommers Diet (Why would you listen to a person who's primary claims to fame are her ability to jiggle and whine through a sitcom that was dumber than her character, and her talent for compressing a modified lever between her thighs?).

3. Diets Named After Geographic Regions:

Mediterranean Diet (Repeat after me, "Goat cheese is an entree."); New Beverly Hills Diet (Paris Hilton and Nicole Ritchie puking in a bathroom as opposed to the Old Beverly Hills diet, which had Irene Ryan and Nancy Kulp feasting on possum.); Cambridge Diet (because nobody wants to eat what the English cook); Sonoma Diet (featuring Ernest and Julio Gallo's Diet Cabernet in a box!); South Beach Diet (where you're shamed into not eating after spending time watching Floridians from that area romping around in their thongs); and the Miami Diet (different from the South Beach diet because, well, okay, it's not different at all).

4. Diets That Are Numerical:

3 Hour Diet (the good news: you eat every three hours, the bad news: you don't get much uninterrupted sleep); 1000 Calorie Diet (because you can only have 1000 calories); 1500 Calorie Diet (because you can only have 1500 calories); 2000 Calorie Diet (because—oh, forget it).

5. Diets that Sound Very Medicinal:

Volumetrics (paging L. Ron Hubbard); Web MD Weight Loss (dating on the Internet; okay, medical advice, not so much); New Mayo Clinic Diet (their slogan? "Diet, or end up here."); Heart Healthy Diet (You mean I can't smoke to stay thin?); Blood Type Diet (You know those homeless guys who sell their blood for a few bucks? Ever see a fat one?); Detox Diet (See Paris Hilton reference in section 3.); Gall Bladder Diet (favored by Zombies); Advocare Diet (You only get to eat what your HMO approves.); Macrobiotic Diet (Let microbes do the work for you.); Arthritis Diet (The more your joints creak and ache, the less likely you are to use utensils.); Triglyceride Diet ("Are you a good cholesterol, or a bad cholesterol?"); Fat Flush Diet (for those on Alli or similar meds); Catabolic Diet (no clue); Ketagenic Diet (same); Dr. Adkins Diet (He's dead, you know.); Lactose Intolerant Diet (I do not want to live in a world without cheese.); Acne Diet (I want to live even less in a world without chocolate.).

6. Diets That Defy Categorization:

GI Diet (the military, not the tract); Body For Life (as opposed to "corpse, afterward"); Eat Right For Your Type (suggesting that what works for the tall, dark and handsome does not work for the blonde, buxom and banal); Personality Type Diet (There are more calories in an eclair when eaten by Barbra Streisand than by Celine Dion.); Slim-Fast (which is the idea); Weight Watchers (Please tell me who isn't.); What Color Is Your Diet, Diet (or, How low is your IQ?); Paleolithic Diet (because if it worked for T-Rex, damn it, it'll work for me!); Bland Diet (unnecessarily repetitive); The Dash Diet (see: Fat Flush Diet); Low residue diet (no clue what it is, but it sounds environmentally friendly); Prism Diet (because after a few days of fasting, your hallucinations allow you to see such pretty colors!); Teenage Diet (McDonald's, Taco Bell, and beer on the sly); Hallelujah Diet (You're not on a diet anymore.).

Now please, read what I'm about to write very carefully. I'm going to help every one of you, and I'm going to save you a lot of money.

If you want to lose weight, you have to eat fewer calories.

Shocking, isn't it! While you're sitting down, I'll tell you even more. I know you can handle it.

If you want to lose weight faster, you have to eat fewer calories, and expend more calories.

Take a minute, I know this is a lot to process, and I'm not done. Collect yourselves a bit, breathe deeply, and soldier on.

Now, if there's one thing you humans want to hear less about than not stuffing your faces, it's doing more in the way of exercise. Humans are getting fatter, and your minis are damn near out of control when it comes to being overweight. Depending on your television channel of choice this development can be called:

a.) trend (NBC)

b.) epidemic (CBS)

c.) Godsend (The Food Channel)

d.) damnable lie perpetrated by the left wingers who are advocating for socialized medicine (FOX)

e.) Godsend (Comedy Central)

f.) turn-off (The Playboy Channel)

g.) turn-on (BET)

h.) sign from Allah that the infidels should be wiped off the face of the Earth (Al Jazeera)

i.) reason for a movie-of-the-week (Lifetime)

j.) boon for sweeps week (Oxygen)

I've noticed that the human population has a very curious relationship with exercise, and it is complex and multi-layered. So, once again, I will makes things simple for you, by describing the groups most humans fall into. Identify where you fit, and you're a step closer to self-realization.

GROUP 1: THE TV'S ON, SO I'VE LOST USE OF MY LEGS or THE COMPUTER'S ON, SO I'VE LOST USE OF MY LEGS

This group is rendered into a deep state of chosen paralysis. Best I can figure, it has something to do with the commonality between the mesmerizing images humans receive through the monitors of their appliance of choice. Those who opt for hours in front of the television have elevated the state of being inert into an art form. Many of them have become so far removed from exercise (of either the physical or mental sort) that, if you stare closely enough, you can almost see the fat cells happily multiplying and pushing out against their waist bands on an hourly basis, in direct proportion to the shriveling and disappearance of their brain cells. If you really think about it, it's a delightfully complementary and utilitarian, you should excuse the term, exercise.

The computer screen is not quite as efficient as the television, because some movement is necessary to manipulate the images on the screen. While relegated to the hands and arms (and I'm not going *there*), the dedicated human non-exerciser achieves equal status with his television-seduced brethren because he has opted to spend his non-work-related computer time in place of physical activity.

GROUP 2: IF OSMOSIS IS GOOD ENOUGH FOR PLANTS, IT'S GOOD ENOUGH FOR HUMANS

This group is actually motivated enough to remove

themselves from the couch or computer chair and go to a health club. Once there, they will look at much of the equipment, spend a sweaty five or six minutes on a barely-moving treadmill, find others of their ilk and lean against some of the handily placed equipment and talk to them for long periods of time. Some will spend time in the sauna, take a shower and go home, at which time they will tell anyone who listens that they spent an hour and a half at the gym today.

GROUP 3: I DON'T KNOW WHY I'M NOT LOSING ANY WEIGHT

These are people who work 9-5 jobs, and use fifteen minutes of their lunch break to walk. The other fifteen minutes, they eat potato chips. And drink coffee. With sugar. And cream. Lots of cream.

GROUP 4: THIRTY MINUTES, THREE TIMES A WEEK IS A LIE

This group has figured out that it takes more than the above prescription to maintain good physical health.

They go to the gym anywhere from three to four times a week, spend the time wisely balancing aerobic work with weight work, doing so to benefit their heart health and well-being, and feel good about themselves as a result.

GROUP 5: I DID IT, SO CAN YOU!

These are former fatties who can't wait to brag about how much weight they've lost, how much more toned they are, how hard they work, blah blah blah. They preach more than convicted politicians who've found religion.

GROUP 6: THERE'S A MIRROR! THERE'S A MIRROR!

These are gym *poseurs* who spend every waking minute they are not at work in a gym, or training for a marathon. They steal furtive looks at themselves in the mirror as soon as they think no one's looking, and every time they do, someone sees them and reacts with a bemused shake of the head. Thankfully, they are so lost in their own egos that they never pick up on how foolishly obvious they are. When out socially, this group does not eat so much as they nibble, and after a meal consisting of three pieces of a spinach leaf, a single bite from a chicken breast, and a glass of Evian, they complain that they feel bloated.

GROUP 7: THE "I REALLY DON'T EXERCISE" MUTANTS

These are naturally fit humans who are simultaneously genetically pre-disposed to be drop-dead gorgeous, and hated by the other 98.6 percent of the human population.

🐾 🐾 🐾

No matter what group you fall into, here's Ruby's easy-to-remember guide to staying fit:

If you want to lose weight and keep it off, you must continue to exercise, continue to watch what you eat, and use common sense while doing both. Your entire life. Period.

I know many of you are stunned, I know many of you are shattered. But you needed to hear it, and from who better than me? I know I've disappointed all of you who want to keep throwing money at Jenny Craig and the estate of Dr. Adkins, or who'd like to continue hoarding grapefruit or cabbage soup.

But it can all be replaced by, you guessed it, *Miss Ruby's Sure Fire Steps to a Leaner You!* Just clip and save:

1. Find a way to exercise more. It doesn't have to be a lot, just more. (Just a thought, walk the canine a little more. Or, if you have a cat, use it for a spirited game of backyard soccer.)
2. Eat a little less. If you eat a little too much one day, eat a little less the next. It's called "moderation."
   Repeat after me, "moderation." Too much food on your plate, cut some off, give it to your canine.
3. Don't allow yourself to get too hungry. Make time to have breakfast, have a nice little healthy snack mid-morning, have a smaller lunch, have an earlier dinner, and a refreshingly light dessert. With the money you save from buying less food, you can purchase a brand new toy for your canine and eventually a new house with a bigger yard for you and your canine to play in and work off more calories.

Remember, the more money you spend on your pet, the less you'll have to spend on all of those offensive calories.

> *The average dog is a nicer person than the average person.*
> Andy Rooney

CHAPTER SEVEN

THE KINDNESS OF STRANGERS

It was not long before the rest of my babies were gone. Matthew was the last, and as the oldest and the toughest, he put up the biggest stink of any of them. I think since he was the last he knew it was inevitable. The staff had already gotten him used to a collar and had begun training him to walk on a leash, but when they took him out that last time, he clamped down on that leash and lay down on the floor.

Didn't budge an inch. He was a pretty chunky fellow by then, with a very dark coat and a white underbelly, and when he decided he wasn't going to move, little short of help straight from the John Deere factory would have gotten the job done. But he was not going to win, and they did move him. He whined the entire way out. That sound is the last piece of my kids that I hold on to.

I was alone now, and my attitude about humans was little changed. The only real act of kindness I'd received that asked for nothing in return had come from the trooper. Mama's human had betrayed me by selling me off to the Beverly Hillbillies, the shelter staff took my kids from me and gave them to who-knows-who. (And I'm sure for a tidy profit.) There was only one worker amongst the shelter staff who I would even let so much as pet me, and when one of them took me out for my daily "exercise" (oh thank you so verrrry much for walking me a whole five minutes a day!), I spent the entire walk looking back at the human on the other end of the leash, sure that at any moment they were going to inflict some sort of humiliation upon me. How could I not be at least a little concerned that they weren't stealthily carrying firecrackers? And frankly, always gnawing at the back of my mind was the possibility that my former human could find me.

All of these factors led me to behaviors that, while born of self-preservation, didn't exactly make me candidate-of-the-month for adoption into a stable home. At first when my babies were gone, the steady flow of onlookers continued, each of them trying to coax me into the adorably warm behavior that they associated with beagles. My reaction? I curled up, my back to them, occasionally glancing their way over my shoulder, shivering with fear. While this place I was in wasn't exactly paradise, at least I wasn't being hit. And frankly, through the filter of my past, I assumed that every human being peering at me through the chain link fence was a candidate to be the next Mike Tyson in my life.

As the weeks passed, interest in me faded to a trickle, and soon, days would pass without a single stranger requesting to take me for a test spin around the exercise yard. I'd overheard what the staff was saying, both to visitors and amongst themselves.

"Yes, she's going to be a lot of work. She was beaten, and we think maybe worse. But she's an intelligent dog and with a little patience …"

"No, I can't say she'll be good with kids."

"She definitely does not like cats."

"If you have another dog, I don't think she'd be a good fit."

"We may not be able to adopt this one out. We're running out of time, really only ten days before we have to put her down."

You know what? That didn't bother me very much at all. When I'd had my little epiphany, my discovery of what real freedom was back when my kids started getting adopted, it occurred to me how little of my life was mine to determine. I'd given birth to five beautiful kids who I now pictured in great homes with big yards, lots of food, and lots of love. That was something, wasn't it? Wasn't that a wonderful legacy to leave? And if I'd had to choose between the big sleep and going back to my former human, well, stick the needle in and let the fluids flow.

But as with so much of what had already happened in my life, this next phase would not come down to my choice. For the second time in my life, a human kindness would be extended my way that would forever change my destiny.

There was no clock within eyesight of the kennel that I had been calling home, so the days and weeks had melted together. I wasn't sure how long it had been since they'd taken the last of my brood from me. Just as I was beginning to accept the inevitable (and Elizabeth Kubler Ross be damned, I accelerated right past the other four stages and went directly into "acceptance") a flurry of activity caught my attention.

The scent hit me first. It was the trooper. No doubt about it. That particular combination of gunpowder and Brylcreem (who knew they still sold that stuff?) was unique to him. When the outside door opened, he entered the room along with two staff regulars. One, the intake worker who first scooped me out of his car, came right to my kennel door and unlatched it. I immediately fled to the farthest regions of the cubicle.

"This is your lucky day, little girl."

Trust me, you've never lived until you've seen a five foot one, 185-pound human female attempting to wedge herself into a chain-link kennel. Water bowl spills, kibble is splattered to and fro. But I was up as far as I could be against the back edge of the fencing, and she was still able to loop one of her thick fingers through my collar, clasping a leash through its ring.

"You're going for a ride now, sweetie."

Ride! I always liked that word. There was some sort of positive connotation to it. At my first human's house, going for a ride usually meant a trip to the vet, and frankly getting a shot and/or being felt up by the same guy entrusted to diagnose horse diseases beat the hell out of getting beat the hell out of.

The hardest thing about having a wagging tail is that there is no way to hide your joy. Sort of like a human male erection. It's direct irrefutable evidence of what the owner is feeling. Human females have it easier. They can always explain away hard nipples because it's cold or because there was a particularly exhilarating breeze. I didn't really want any of the humans to know how or what I was feeling, but "ride" sent an involuntary tingle straight to my back side, and sent me into the canine version of the Beyonce booty bump.

"Oh look. She wants to go for a ride!"

I told you.

The rotund female human led me to the front counter of the shelter where she gave the trooper some instructions and had him sign a form or three. "I think," she said to him as he took the lead and began walking towards the exit, "this is an amazing thing you're doing."

The trooper just shrugged. Oooh, the tall, silent type! Just like my Ralph. I followed him, still reluctantly, not knowing what was going on. He opened a door on the cruiser, and I leapt in, walking to the passenger side of the car. "Okay girl," he began. "We're going to go for a long ride." (There was the magic word again! Thank goodness I hadn't seen even a single episode of *The Sopranos* yet.) "See, if no one was going to adopt you, that meant that they were going to have to put you down." He extended his big mitt of a hand and scratched at the back of my neck. I'd never been a big one on being petted, and I cringed a bit, but I trusted this guy so I didn't fight too hard.

"So you have to behave, because we're going to be driving for about two and a half hours. I'm going to take you to Chicago, to a place where they won't kill dogs. But before we go, I'm getting pretty tired of calling you 'girl.' So we're going to give you a name."

I had a name. My Mama gave it to me. And it certainly wasn't that dreadful 'Bitsy.' But I couldn't communicate that yet. I had no computer access.

"Ruby. From here on out, I'm going to call you Ruby."

Could have been worse. Certainly a step up from Bitsy. Then again "Schlomo" would have been a step up from that.

The trooper put the car into gear, and as we pulled out of the lot, I sat in the passenger seat, staring at the passing scene, mesmerized, acting as if I was ignoring everything he said. It didn't discourage him though, and he kept talking. "Ruby. Ruby was my dog's name when I was a little boy. She was a mutt, but the same colors as you. Brown, black, a lot of white. Miss Ruby was the best. I'd come home from school, Ruby was waiting for me. I had two brothers and two sisters, but Ruby didn't pay them any attention at all when I was around. She slept on my feet in winter, woke me up for school every morning, and snored louder than my Granny. She was with me for sixteen years. Had the very same big brown eyes like you. No one ever gave me the kind of love my Ruby gave me. No one. I love my wife and she loves me, but she's allergic so I can't keep you with me. Now I can tell someone beat the tar out of you Ruby. And maybe this sounds a little crazy, but somehow, I can't help but think if I make sure you get some of the same love Ruby gave me, it'll be the best way for me to keep my Ruby's memory alive. You understand, girl?"

I understood.

I kept acting happily distracted by the passing kaleidoscope of images whizzing past us as he drove down the highway. But I got it.

I was profoundly lucky to have been found by this kind human, this enormous kind human with his enormous kind heart. "Ruby" wasn't a name to him. It was a legacy. I stayed on the passenger side of the car for a long time. He didn't say another word. My eyes got heavy after an hour or so, and I curled up and fell asleep. When I awoke, it was because of a delicious smell. The trooper was at a Burger King drive thru.

After receiving his bag full of aromatic goodies, he pulled the car over, and took out a burger. I stood, tail hopelessly wagging, staring. Rude, yes. But can you blame me? He broke off a little bit of the sandwich and held it out to me. I wanted to lunge for it, but I needed to do something first. I moved right past his outstretched hand, raised my neck up, and gave him a kiss on his stubbly cheek.

∴ ∴ ∴

By the time we arrived at our destination, night had fallen. As it turned out, this place wasn't in Chicago, it was outside Chicago by about fifteen miles. When the trooper stopped the car, he told me to stay put and he went inside. I looked around. Not bad. Nice enough building. An animal hospital was directly adjacent to it.

There was a nice-sized field on the other side of the hospital along with what looked like an outdoor penned area. That must be where the inmates were allowed to go for exercise.

The trooper returned, opened the driver's side door and reached across to take hold of my leash. He tugged at it, and I followed, but before I could jump out of the car, he grabbed my head and held it between his palms. "My Ruby." And he kissed me on the forehead.

As he led me into the new shelter, I looked around and tried to take it all in. The entranceway was crammed, mountains of newspapers forming artificial walls lining the hallway. No sooner had I taken a single step inside, than I was accosted by that singularly wretched smell, that most vile, offensive, unspeakable odor of the creepiest cretins to ever be blessed with fur coats.

Cats. A lot of cats.

We went into a tiny office, where a woman with glasses so thick they looked like she'd gotten them as a gag gift, was furiously typing into a computer.

"Does she have a name?" Her voice was nasal, irritating. She wore her hair pulled back in a functional ponytail that failed to hide the fact that she hadn't shampooed in days. Her attire was almost identical to what the females at the last shelter wore, which was basically hospital issue 1950s kitchen-wallpaper chic.

"Ruby."

"How cute."

Freakin' adorable.

"And do we know how old Ruby is?"

No "we" don't, but I do. So rude to ask about a lady's age anyway. What was the story with her age anyway? By the creases on her forehead, however many years she'd lived had been hard miles indeed.

"Not a clue. I found her by the side of a road."

"Her nipples are still big. Has she given birth?"

Of course I've given birth! That's my excuse. So exactly what's the reason you have an ass the size of Montana?

"Yeah. They adopted out her pups."

"Okay. Well, that about does it. We'll put her in a back cage for the night. She'll be examined tomorrow by a vet and a behaviorist, we'll get her picture on our web site and try to get her a good home as soon as possible. I'll take her now."

The trooper nodded and handed the loop end of the leash over to Mrs. Magoo.

"Okay, Ruby. We're going to take you back to your new home."

I pulled back, resisting, and looked straight up at the trooper, an involuntary whimper escaping from my throat. He turned away quickly, and walked away from me at a pace that was faster than I'd ever seen him move. As the woman pulled harder at my leash, compelling me to follow her, my thoughts were only of the trooper. I knew he was crying. I knew that he was aware that he'd done a wonderful thing. I wanted him to be sure to drive that long way home safely. And I didn't want him to forget me.

I never saw him again.

> *Dogs love their friends and bite their enemies, quite unlike people who are incapable of pure love and always have to mix love and hate.*
> Sigmund Freud

CHAPTER EIGHT

RUBY'S TIPS FOR BETTER LIVING

PART 2: SELF-HELP

THE SECRET ABOUT ... *THE SECRET (please cue mystical soundtrack)*

Author Rhonda Byrne was only telling part of the truth when she discovered ... *The Secret (please cue mystical soundtrack)*. You see, the real secret is to sell the gullible a so-easy-anyone-can-do-it-if-they-just-wish-hard-enough solution to their problems. This is the theory of karma re-packaged in book and DVD form. In the canine world, we call this theory *horseshit*.

There are plenty of very good canines out there who love their owners, are great to them, loyal to a fault. And they still get treated horribly. There are plenty of good humans out there, who've put out positive vibes their entire lives, only to be dumped upon. When you boil it all down, *The Secret (please cue mystical soundtrack)* is telling you to click your heals three times, and keep repeating that there's no place like home ... or there's no home like a mansion ... or there's no job like a higher paying one ... or there's no partner like a better looking one. *The Secret (please cue mystical soundtrack)* infers that if you're not as happy as you want to be, rich as you want to be, loved as you want to be, you haven't clicked those heels hard enough or often enough. But the bottom line is it's your fault. Ms. Byrne is smart enough to tell and sell people exactly what they want to hear.

Yeah, I know this is simplifying it. But you humans who've bought into *The Secret (please cue mystical soundtrack)* apparently need it explained to you in the simplest terms possible.

You want to know the real secret? There is no one secret. What brings each of us happiness is as unique as you are.

THE SECRET (please cue mystical soundtrack) **ABOUT MOTIVATIONAL SPEAKERS**

These guys with the preternatural smiles who charge a small fortune for their seminars are the twenty-first-century version of traveling medicine shows. The elixirs they're selling are just as phony. I'm about to save any of you thinking about signing up for one of these things a lot of money. Pay attention:

1. The best way to be happy is to work at a job that makes you happy.
2. Money doesn't make you happy, but it does save you the worry about money, which can help make you happier.
3. You have to love yourself before others can love you. Why? When you love yourself, you don't NEED to be loved by others, so you won't compromise your definition of love by being sucked into relationships that are toxic. Love becomes what it's supposed to be; a positive force, an inspiring force, of mutual benefit, of equal joy.
4. It is better to give than to receive. So go give your canine an extra treat right now. You'll feel better about yourself.

Trust me.

PETA (PEOPLE FOR THE ETHICAL TREATMENT OF ANIMALS)

As a self-professed emissary of the animal kingdom, I don't want to sound ungrateful. But at the same time, I'm not so sure that the tactics this group uses in the name of defending animals don't make the cause itself look a little loony-tunes, thereby compromising their good intentions. The most basic law of the jungle is "survival of the fittest." We canines accept that. We understand that survival of the fittest means that some animals are going to be used as sources of food and clothing for humans. It seems to me that the forces at PETA don't get that concept as fully as they should. If it's predatory behavior they're after, I have no recollection of PETA pickets set up on some African savannah imploring lions to go on a vegan diet.

I understand and think it's even noble in some instances to discourage wearing fur, but do these people understand that when they throw paint on some celebrity's fur coat, the celebrity goes out and BUYS ANOTHER FUR COAT? So, because I'm all about helping humans, I have an alternate strategy for those of you who are infuriated by the fact that minks, raccoons, sables, etc. often end up keeping the likes of Aretha Franklin warm. (Tempted as I may be, I will not insert a joke here about how many dead minks it would take to keep the Queen of Soul warm. Nor will I offer conjecture as to why a woman with that amount of insulation would need a fur coat to keep warm in the first place. I am above all that. I am not above asking, however, if someone who cares about the woman, legend or not, has ever suggested the salad bar as an option.)

Cats.

Yes, cats. They have fur, they have no redeeming features and no apparent purpose on Earth other than to intimidate rodents. (as I've written earlier, in canine religion, Dog is fallible so we can chalk up cats under the category of "Major Fuck-Ups" right along with the Narwhal, the Corvair, and Alan Keyes running for anything.) You PETA types, while we're at it, if ethical treatment of all animals is so important to you, why not savage cats for their continuing abuse of mice and rats? By using cats as a principal means of producing fur coats, you are really giving them the gift of purposeful life. Yeah, that's it! You've transformed them from being these shadowy creatures who murder defenseless babies in their cribs, munch on rats, show no affection, and whose principal redeeming characteristic is the ability to crap in sand, into a species that serves the greater human good by helping them get through cold spells.

Think of how quickly we could reduce the overcrowding in shelters! Why, with one coat for Miss Franklin alone, we could double the capacity of all the shelters in Detroit!

I'm so ashamed.

> *Don't accept your dog's admiration as conclusive*
> *evidence that you are wonderful.*
> Ann Landers

CHAPTER NINE

A NEW LEAF

I'd only been in this new place two days when he found me. I've already described the surroundings in Chapter 1 (Forget that part already? And you think *we* have a limited attention span.) His attire was, well, rumpled. He was wearing a sweat suit of some sort, hairline receding, patches of gray above each ear, and a nose better suited to an anteater.

I assumed my regular position at the back of the cage when he began talking to me. It wasn't quite that dreaded human baby-talk, but it didn't exactly give me a clue about whether or not he had any semblance of intelligence.

"Well look at this pretty girl. Hey? Hey Ruby. Look at me baby."

I offered a fleeting glance his way.

"Hey girl. How about going for a little walk with me?"

What a line. Yeeesh.

The female worker with the glass-block spectacles opened the gate and unceremoniously dragged me up into her fleshy arms. She carried me into a common room area, and set me down.

"Spend as much time as you want in here getting to know her."

This new male human sat on the couch in the middle of the room, and I basically ignored him, investigating the other dog smells that had been left behind.

I heard a thumping as he heavily patted his hand on the

couch. "Come up here girl, let me see you up here on the couch."

Right. Hop up on the couch, eh. Why? So you can slug me like my first human. I wasn't taking the bait. I'd learned that human furniture was *verboten.*

"All right, then I'll come down by you."

Well, I'll be damned if he didn't lie down on the floor, full out on his stomach, leaning his head on his arms that were folded in front of him. "See girl, nothing to be afraid of."

I kept circling the room, glancing his way, sometimes creeping closer, teasing, but always pulling back any time he moved even so much as a muscle. "It's okay, Ruby. I'm just going to lie here, and you come over whenever you want."

I hope you don't have anything to do the rest of the day, because unless you're carrying some concealed bacon that I can't smell right now, your time on the floor is going to be exclusively solo.

Minutes passed. He didn't budge. Amazing patience. Piqued my curiosity, I must admit. I stared at him for a few minutes, curious. Slowly, I began to move towards him, tentatively, closer to his feet, a safe distance from his arms. He wore tattered Reeboks that smelled of snow and grass. I sniffed at them, and then at his right pant leg. Spaghetti sauce, spilled not too recently. The only movement he betrayed was the rise and fall of his back and chest as he breathed. Pretty impressive. My guard was still up, but I began moving closer to his arms. I kept sniffing, the hair on his arms tickling my nose, forcing an embarrassing sneeze.

"You're a sneezy girl."

And he'd been doing so well. "Sneezy girl!" I mean,

honestly.

Undeterred, I moved closer to his face. His chin was resting on his arms, his nose an inviting target. I approached it gently, and brushed my nose against it ever so slightly, careful not to use my tongue and make him think I might be open to warmth. No kisses at first sight from this canine. Still, the only movement, the only sound was from his breathing.

I took one more quick pass at him, only to be interrupted by the sound of the door.

"Well, what do you think?" asked Nurse Ratched.

The human male started to get up. "She's a beautiful girl."

Score one point for Cyrano.

"What do you know about her background?" he asked.

The human female gave him the whole trooper story. "Amazing," he whispered. He looked at me. "I think you and I have a lot in common, young lady."

I'm listening.

"I don't think she'd be good with other dogs or cats," croaked the woman.

"I don't have any other pets," he replied. "And I hate cats."

WE HAVE A WINNER!

"Okay, Ruby. I think you're going to be my dog."

This was really sudden, and I didn't know quite what to feel about the whole deal. I'd spent so much time at the other place, and here I was, just a day or two, and someone was ready to take me home. Granted the entire process is pretty barbaric. Let's recap, shall we? I'm kept in a cage with a cold cement floor, a bowl of water, and a little contraption that looks like a mini-trampoline that passes for the canine version of an army cot. I'm in one of twelve kennels in this place, and the racket is interminable. Even the hint of an opened door anywhere within earshot spurs the other canines into an orgiastic howl-fest that is just as unpleasant for me to hear as it would be for any pet-intolerant human.

You don't want to know about the smell. Unfortunately, my fellow inmates were not as discreet about taking care of their business as I was. Try this for an analogy: how would you like to live in a multi-unit apartment complex that had fencing instead of walls? Think you'd see and smell a lot more than you'd want to?

So who was I sharing this space with? Directly across the room from me was Ivan. He was a Shepherd mix, about fifty pounds. One of his eyes was grotesquely clouded with a cataract. He'd been in this place for over a year. Can you imagine? A year sleeping on cement. He'd pace all day, circling his kennel, occasionally lapping at his water bowl. Truth be told, I think he'd lost touch with reality.

There were two pit bulls. One, Daisy, was two cages down from me, and the other, Brutus was at the far end of the room. I know, "Daisy" the pit bull. Kind of like naming a piranha "Mother Teresa." But Daisy seemed like a very laid back girl. Never barked. Rumor had it that she'd turned on her owner.

She never talked about it and I didn't ask. It's always the quiet ones. Brutus had shoulders like a middle linebacker. Not an ounce of fat on him. Black as coal. Hmmmm. I never got to spend any real time with him, but if I could have, let's just say that young man would have known the true meaning of "doggy style."

There was a noisy Pointer, an elderly Lab whose human had died, four ever-chattering Chihuahuas (unparalleled ability to irritate made me rethink my opinion of no-kill shelters), a male Beagle (younger than I, unmannered and ill-bred), and a Huskie with the most mesmerizing steel-blue eyes I've ever seen.

The Huskie was there because the family who'd bought her thought she was beautiful, but didn't realize how much work and attention the breed needed. How utterly unlike you humans to judge a being solely on its appearance.

Granted, we did have free medical, something you American humans can't quite seem to figure out. But even that did little to rationalize the conditions we were living under. Look, I was the lucky one here. I'd been rescued from certain death—twice—and I was in this place less than seventy-two hours when someone wanted to take me home. Yet, was I allowed to have any say in this deal? No. Was I allowed even so much as a chance to see where my next home was going to be before being relocated? No.

I was being treated like a Katrina survivor.

Two days passed before my new human returned. The staff had me bathed (against my will, I hate the feel of water against my fur) and primped, nails clipped (also by force, don't like anyone messing with my paws), and fitted with a nice new collar. When one of the attendants came to get me and bring me to the front of the shelter, the other canines I left behind all wished me well, the howls echoing off the concrete block walls. As I walked out, I took one last glance back at poor Ivan. He hadn't even looked my way, lost in his maniacal routine of circling his cage.

I often wonder if he's still there.

My new human was waiting for me, and he looked genuinely pleased when the supervisor handed my leash over to him.

"Congratulations. I'm sure you're going to make a wonderful home for her. And don't forget the appointment."

"It's already been made."

Appointment? Well, I didn't pay much attention.

"Okay, Ruby, we're going to go to your new home."

How could I be anything but skeptical?

"Aw, your tail's between your legs. It's going to be okay, really. Come on now."

And with that, he led me across the parking lot to his car. I knew what that meant. RIDE! As exciting as that prospect was, I did a great job of restricting my tail's movement, and simply jumped in the car as soon as he opened the door. The car was a big flesh-colored monstrosity, newly purchased based on the smell. I walked to the passenger side and heard him click his seat belt. Looking out the window, feigning indifference to him, I have to say I was sort of happy that my paws, dampened with traces of snow, had left a print or two on the car's upholstery.

"Okay, Ruby, here we go."

He slipped the car into gear, and it jostled me just a bit off balance. I recovered quickly though, kept my cool. I knew instinctively that I had to show who was going to be boss here, and I didn't want to betray any sign of even the slightest weakness. This was a challenge though, because frankly I was terrified of what could be. As he turned out of the parking lot, I knew it was time to be assertive. Looked to me like the scenery on the driver's side was more interesting than what was on my side of the car, so I simply stepped across the seat and towards the driver's-side window. Of course, that meant stepping on him and in front of him as he steered.

"Um, careful now girl. I have to see where I'm going."

This is a test. You are now being tested by the emergency canine navigating system. This is only a test. Had this been a major commercial thoroughfare, I would have kept my hairy butt on the passenger's side of the car.

"Okay now, girl. You have to go to the other side of the car while I drive."

Was he assuming I understood what he was saying? Must have, because he didn't use his free hand to move me or direct me away. Of course I did understand what he was saying, but he couldn't know that. So I stood there. For the entire ride home. I was quite proud of myself.

After about ten minutes, he drove the car down a quiet lane. On either side of the road were very sing-song, quaint, suburban townhouses. The trees were still barren with the cold of late February, but it looked nice enough. My current human pulled the car into a narrow driveway. "Here we are Ruby. Your new home."

It was, well, pleasant, in a planned-community-everything-looks-the-same sort of way. Light tan garage doors with siding that matched, and forest green border trim. The sidewalk was shoveled with some care, a thin bed of fresh snow covered the tiny lawn in front of the cement steps that led to the home's entrance. My human (whose name I was still unaware of) led me out of the car. I followed, warily. While I had a bad vibe about my last human owner, I had nothing substantial to base that same premonition on with this one.

Vibe or not, I would not forget that I hadn't really known what I was going to be in for from my first owner until I was actually in his home and subjected to his relentless onslaught.

I expected to go right into the house, but my new human took a detour, and decided to go for a short walk (which he would dub "short walkies," as opposed to what would become our noon and five PM, six- to ten-block journeys known as "long walkies") around the cul-de-sac. I walked several paces ahead of him, glancing back, keeping a watchful eye, half-expecting to be struck at any moment. I admit that was due to my paranoia more than anything he had done or shown thus far, but we were actually only minutes into this profoundly imbalanced relationship, so who could blame me?

"Wanna go potty, girl?" he kept asking as we short-walkied.

I did, but I sorta didn't want to give him the satisfaction, so I held off for a bit, and finally went on my own terms, at my own timing, in a bush of my choice. That may not seem like much to you, but believe me, to a canine any time we can make a choice about anything, it feels like victory. As an aside, it's pretty mortifying to have to urinate under the watchful eyes of a human. That's why I never make eye contact with one while I'm going. Thank goodness for yards where we are afforded a level of privacy that you humans take for granted. I have to admit I was anxious to see my new yard.

"Oh, good girl Ruby."

Giveaway! "Praise the dog when it eliminates" is straight out of every dog-care manual known to man, so I knew what that meant.

I was his first canine. Good Dog, I was dealing with a virgin pet owner. This was not going to be easy.

We rounded the block and returned to where we'd started. He opened the door, and I got my first look at what was his home, and what would become *our* home. Their was a carpeted flight of about twelve steps. Good sign, I liked carpet. If I had to sleep on the floor, at least it would be somewhat comfortable.

He slipped off his gym shoes and bent down to pet me. (I would come to learn that when he bought new sneaks, he would tie them in a bow loose enough so that he could just slip them on and off at will without having to tie them again. This, of course, is the height of laziness. He may as well have just gone with velcro.)

"I'm going to keep you on the leash Ruby. Come on, we're going to take a tour of the house."

I followed him up the steps, and I have to say the carpet felt glorious under my paws. Warm, soft, so—so *not* cement. When I got to the top of the stairs, I was stunned. The walls were covered, and I mean from baseboard to ceiling, with hockey memorabilia. For a minute, I thought I'd be living in a sporting goods store. To my left was a nice little dinette set. Just beyond that were sliding glass doors that led to a small balcony. Ahead of me was an overstuffed, very inviting couch. Tempting, but I remembered my place as reinforced by my first human. My new human led me forward, and took me towards my right. There was a tiny, serviceable kitchen. It was clear by this time that this guy was the only human in the house. There were no other smells of note besides his. What was troubling was I was now standing in the kitchen area, and I wasn't smelling any food.

What the hell did that mean?

I didn't have much time to ponder (and yes, we dogs ponder, as if you all cornered the market on Socratic reasoning) as he led me towards the back area of the place. We went down a tiny hall and through a door to my left. Here was an office, standard desk, computer, phone. The walls in here were covered as well. But it wasn't hockey stuff this time, it was all posters, photos, and album covers related to Motown in general and Diana Ross in particular.

This was one peculiar human.

After taking a spin around that room, he led me off to my right and into the bedroom. There was an inviting looking crate-carrier with its gate open that beckoned to me. Its floor was lined with thick terry cloth towels, and as far as I was concerned, it may as well have been the Presidential Suite at the Ritz. Just ahead of it was a brand spanking new deep brick-red "doggy bed." It was lined with an ochre fleece. Very inviting.

His bed was huge, king-size, and dominated the room. More importantly for me, there was a nice space between the wall and the bottom of the headboard, a gap that looked like it might make a great refuge in case my human ever wanted to go Michael Vick on my ass. Attached directly to the bedroom was an enormous bathroom, and when we walked in there, my paws made that neat little clicking sound of nails against the tile.

Now I should tell you that throughout this guided tour, I never once showed any stereotypical canine interest in my human. I kept my nose to the carpet, sniffing to ferret out as much information as I could gather, and only looked at him to make sure I wasn't going to be hit. The leash he had was a short one, so I couldn't do a lot of independent investigation.

"Now Ruby, I'm going to let you stay in the bedroom here for a little while so you can get comfortable with the house one room at a time."

See! Another hint from the how-to-handle-your-new-dog manual.

With that, he pulled a safety-gate out of a closet, placed it across the bedroom doorway, reached down to unclasp my leash, and left the room. As soon as I was free from the leash, I made a mad dash for the safety that I felt I was sure to find underneath the bed. I listened carefully for several minutes. Breathing, but no movement. I crawled back out, and peered around. I was indeed, alone in this room. Immediately, I went to the crate. It smelled human-clean. That's not a good thing for us canines. We want a little earthiness to our surroundings, that lived-in smell. I stepped all the way into the crate, and liked it. I really liked it. The towels were heavenly beneath me, the epitome of luxury. Cathedral ceiling was a plus. Having completed that inspection, I walked further around the room. Getting to the safety gate, I had a direct view into the den area, and there sat my new human. He was reading something, or fake-reading something, waiting to see my next move.

"Hi Ruby. You're a good girl."

I still didn't know if I could trust him, but he sure was easy to please. So I doubled back and kept sniffing around the room. The smells of the carpeting around the bed gave me no information. The only scent I could really pick up was his, confirming my earlier thoughts about his domestic situation. I don't know why it hit me at this moment, but something suddenly dawned on me. This place, this house. There was the front entrance, there was the sliding door to the balcony. But we walked up steps when we came into the house, so the balcony must be on a second level. That means—

NO! NO dear Dog! It can't be!

I WAS LIVING IN A HOUSE THAT HAD NO YARD!

A barking dog is often more useful than a sleeping lion.
Washington Irving

CHAPTER TEN

SECRETS AND LIES

In this chapter, I thought I'd take the opportunity to write about a lot of loose ends, starting with the mistaken beliefs people hold about the animal world in general and canines in particular. So let's have at some of the biggest misconceptions:

DOGS DON'T KNOW IF YOU'RE AWAY FROM THEM FOR FIVE HOURS OR FIVE DAYS.

This is one of those things scientists came up with. Humans with canines can witness for themselves the difference in reaction to them when they see a canine after being at work all day ("Happy to see you, here's some kisses, now take me outside so I can take a leak!"), as opposed to when they've been on vacation for ten days ("Thank Dog! Finally! Now get me the hell out of this smelly kennel and away from these cretin flea bags and back to my couch!").

Here's a thought for the scientists and their methodologies: When you're gone for an hour and you come back, you're a scientist coming back into our daily routine. When you're gone for ten days and you come back, you're a scientist coming back into our daily routine. It's not about our reaction, it's about our reaction to YOU.

DOGS ARE COLOR BLIND

We're not. So when you dress badly, we know it.

THE REAL TRUTH ABOUT CATS AND DOGS

Here it is in a nutshell: cats are despicable creatures that were the end result of ritual genetic experiments conducted by the ancient Mayans. I think LSD was involved, but that's just conjecture on my part.

IT'S RAINING CATS AND DOGS

It's never rained cats and dogs. That's just some weird human metaphor. It has, however, rained frogs.

Don't believe me? Go rent *Magnolia*. Great movie, a little out there, but there's a scene with Tom Cruise in his underwear. He was also in his underwear in *Risky Business*. And *All The Right Moves*. How'd I get onto this subject?

AS LONG AS I'M TALKING ABOUT TOM CRUISE (WHO'S NOT, I REPEAT, NOT GAY), THERE IS NO HOMOSEXUALITY IN THE ANIMAL KINGDOM

Maybe not while you're looking. But folks, seriously. Think of all of the two-canine households you know. Most of them have canines of the same gender. Coincidence? I think not. The real giveaway? Take a look at what lines their crates. If it's Martha Stewart sheets, I think you know the deal.

A DOG IS HAPPY IF IT'S WAGGING ITS TAIL

Most canines are happy if our tails are wagging. *Most*. But be warned, every so often, rarely, yes, but they are out there, there are canines who wag their tails in a deliberate attempt to lull and lure a random human.

And once they get close enough, once they get comfortable

enough, once the canine hears, "Oh, what a good boy," he lunges at the human's jugular, teeth piercing the flesh, blood flying, as the victim chokes out a gurgling, horrific scream!

Okay, none of that is true. I was just trying to test you. See, my next book is going to be in the horror genre. Working title? *Die Charles Grodin, Die!: The Revenge of Beethoven.*

DOGS LOOK LIKE THEY'RE SMILING, BUT THEY CAN'T REALLY SMILE

Where do you get this nonsense? Of course canines smile. We laugh too. Do you think comedians are confined to the world of the homo sapiens? Let me give you an example. Remember this old joke coined by a human comedian circa 1962?

Q: Why does a dog lick its balls?
A: Because it can.

Well, there's a rising star making the circuit at the canine comedy clubs named Great Dane Cook. I grant you he's derivative, but here's his take on the same joke:

Q: Why do humans use their hands to masturbate?
A: Because they can.

While I'm on the topic of canine-centered entertainment, I will tell you that there is such a thing as for-canine-ears-only media. No, I'm not going to contend that we have some secret television station that telecasts shows aimed at the canine demographic. Thanks to the generosity of the folks who came up with cable's *Animal Planet* and CNN (Canine Network

News), that's not necessary. But as you may be aware, we have a super-acute sense of hearing, which is how we've been able to enjoy our own radio station. The programming is as varied as our species. We have music that caters to the young pups in the hood, featuring the best-selling canine artist of this century, Snoop-Human. Maybe I'm showing my age, but I personally can't stand him. Too much use of the M-word for me. My ancestors did not endure their epic struggle for freedom only to hear others refer to themselves and each other as "mutts."

Disgusting.

And speaking of disgusting, I also don't care for the station's most popular talk show, *The Jerry Springer Spaniel Show*. To me, it's just a showcase for our basest behavior and caters to the worst prurient interests of our species. How many times can someone watch two bitches fighting over a weiner dog? It's as close as we come to acting like, well, dare I say it, poor-bred humans.

I'm partial to uplifting stories; Dalmatians and how they work with firemen, German Shepherds who lead the blind, Beagles who sniff for drugs at the airport, Labs who search for survivors in building wreckage, Shih Tzus who have to act in lieu of starlets' brains. Unfortunately, like our human counterparts, good news doesn't sell like the sensational, but I still appreciate the fact we have our own station. And it should not be a mystery as to what outlet carries it. Why, Sirius, of course.

HUMANS DON'T CHOOSE THEIR DOGS, DOGS CHOOSE THEIR HUMANS

Only in a perfect world.

STEREOTYPES CANINES HAVE ABOUT HUMANS

While I realize a lot of what I've written is canine-centric (What else would you expect?), I will take my own species to task for reducing and categorizing humans based on the behaviors of a few. So here are some commonly held beliefs in the canine world.

CANINES ARE TERRITORIAL BUT HUMANS ARE PSYCHOTICALLY TERRITORIAL

This belief would imply that humans would go to any length, even murderous warfare, to lay claim to something as relatively insignificant as where one border ends and another begins. I wonder how we ever got that idea?

HUMANS HAVE A GREATER GRASP OF THE ARTS THAN CANINES

No canine ever wrote, or danced to a Polka. No canine every paid millions of dollars for a painting of a bunch of soup cans. No canine has ever, of his free will, seen a Pauly Shore movie.

HUMANS HAVE A GREATER INTELLECTUAL CAPACITY THAN CANINES

Two words: *National Enquirer.*

After further review, I guess canines do not hold unfair stereotypes about humans. You guys might want to try and change that.

The factory of the future will have only 2 employees, a man and a dog. The man will be there to feed the dog. The dog will be there to keep the man from touching the equipment.

Warren Brunis

CHAPTER ELEVEN

NO PLACE LIKE HOME

The horror of the realization that I had been sentenced to a house with no yard was gut wrenching. No place to exercise, no place for the slightest expression of freedom, and most humiliatingly, no privacy in matters of waste management. I was doomed to tailor my bowel movements around the conveniences of this strange, large-nosed human whose house was decorated with equal parts hockey, books and Motown, and whose kitchen did not have any discernible smell of food.

I felt like I was trapped in a Coen Brothers movie.

That first day, my new human must have taken me around the cul-de-sac eight different times. I could sense that he feared I was going to violate his carpet if he didn't. What, did he think I was raised by wolves? After the second trip, he gave me my first treat, a Milk Bone cookie. It was delicious, and I quickly became addicted.

But I fought the pangs of desire for more, because I was still unsure of what was and wasn't unacceptable behavior, and that included how to ask for another cookie. After my third spin around the block, he filled a blue bowl with dried food and set it down in the living room next to a matching blue bowl of crystal clear water. It was the same food they gave me at the shelter, and I was sure, just as tasteless. I didn't even sniff at it, and didn't go near the water.

"Ruby, here's dinner. Be a good girl and have your dinner."

Still on the leash, he led me closer to the bowls. "Go on,

have your dinner." He unclasped the leash, and the moment I heard the click confirming that I was free, I tore off into the bedroom and took refuge under the bed.

"No, Ruby, don't be afraid. I just want you to have dinner."

And I just want to make sure that if I get full, I'll have a chance to deal with the eventual aftermath with a little privacy and dignity. I did not want to have some odd human eyeballing my most personal functions. I mean seriously, how utterly gross.

"Ruby, come out from under there."

I scrunched back as far as my body would let me (I was still carrying a few extra pounds courtesy of my kids), and he began reaching in, attempting to gain control of my collar. He had no idea how vulnerable he was. His hand, sitting right there, totally unprotected. I could have let the anger I felt about the yard situation overtake me. I could have clamped down into that soft pink human flesh and felt oh so satisfied, even if it was for a moment.

But I didn't. I knew the fate of others of my kind who'd lashed out mindlessly if instinctively at an impending threat.

Without benefit of due process, they'd been tried, convicted, and executed by human kangaroo courts. Odd that humans, the most violent creatures on Dog's green Earth, are so quick to destroy behavior that too often mimics their own. The mirror can be a most frightening place to look. So I just held my tongue and held my ground. I could see his face, distorted, right cheek pressed into the carpet, tilted to one side so he could see under the bed. His arm kept flailing as he grabbed at my collar, but I was safely out of reach. After another minute or so, he left. I heard him walk away, heard shuffling from what

I assumed was the kitchen area, and then steps coming back my way.

"Ruby, you cannot stay under that bed. Now, I'm not going to hit you with this. But you need to come here."

And with that, a long yellow broom handle swept its way towards me. He moved it slowly. If he had wanted to, he could have hurt me with that, but to his credit, he didn't. Slowly, deliberately, he manipulated it until it was within inches of me. I was fearful, I admit. I'd been struck with a broom at my first human's, and I was familiar with the sting, an experience I was not anxious to revisit. I began to move away, knowing that if I continued to do so, I would have to leave the protection the bed afforded me. My reflexes were good, and while my pregnancy had left me a step slower than I'd been, I decided that maybe I could make a break for the crate. So just a split second before the stick made contact with me, I bolted from underneath the bed, and tore around the room heading for the crate.

He was waiting for me. Before I knew it, he had wrapped both of his arms around me and was picking me up.

"It's okay, Ruby. I just want you to eat some dinner. I'm not going to hurt you, I know you're scared, but you cannot go under the bed again.."

I did not make a sound, I did not look at him. I did try and wriggle my way out of his arms, but he was too strong. He brought me to the food bowl, placed me down and held tight.

"Dinner, baby. Have some dinner. Be a good girl."

Just as he finished that sentence, his grip loosened ever so slightly and before he knew it, I was back under the bed.

"BAD GIRL!" he screamed as he took off after me. "NO!"

I expected to get round two of the broom, but several

minutes passed, and nothing. I heard footsteps, but nothing coming close to the bedroom. Then, a smell. Faint at first, but unmistakable. The scent got stronger, more seductive.

Milk Bone cookie. DAMN YOU HUMAN! DAMN YOU TO HELL!

Sure enough, there it was. Right at the doorway, lying there all innocent, practically begging to be eaten. But the smell was stronger than one cookie. Yes! Beyond that cookie was another, and then another.

Good Dog! He'd left me a veritable yellow brick road of cookies that stretched to the Oz of the food bowl. What to do? He was expecting me to be weak, to cave in. And there he was, sitting back on the couch, all smug and self-congratulatory for having laid this foolproof trap. From that distance, there was no way he was going to be able to grab me. I was sure to get at least two cookies before he could get close. So I began to inch out from under the bed. I stared at my opponent the entire time. He didn't move at all. I was within easy reach now, so I lunged, grabbed the cookie and retreated to the safety the bed provided, expecting the human to be fast on my tail. As I settled back to enjoy my prey, I looked back up, and he hadn't moved.

Hmmm. Puzzling.

This pattern repeated itself when I went after the second cookie, and the third. The fourth was only feet from where he sat. Dare I make such a bold attempt? The cookies were so good. And I had been so hungry.

I peered back out at him, and he did the oddest thing. He lay down on the couch. Was this some ingenious trap? Was he lulling me into a false sense of security before pouncing on me and beating me into submission? If that was the case, it was going to happen sooner or later. So I went for it. He didn't move. I got the cookie, ran back under the bed, looked up, and there he was, still prone on the couch. He didn't say a word. No "good girl," no "bad girl." Nothing. That fourth cookie left me thirsty. I knew that cool dish of water was out there, but I'd already gotten away with four cookies safely, I didn't want to push it.

Besides, the anxiety of the day was exhausting. I was getting sleepy. I would have been fine under that bed, but the soft lining of the crate beckoned. Cautiously, I made my way from under the bed and into the crate. I was still pretty keyed up, but desperately wanted sleep. Then, I heard the footsteps. He was coming into the room, and I was in the crate, vulnerable. I peered up through the slats of the ceiling and saw him look down at me. I expected him to confront me, to reach into the crate and drag me out for another tour of the cul-de-sac, or perhaps my first beating at his hands.

But he just lay down on his bed. He rolled over on his side, stared at me, and whispered, "It's okay, Ruby. I love you."

Who was this guy?

The next day was largely a repeat of the first. The cat and mouse game (an analogy I do not like using, as you might guess) continued. He found a way to break the dinner stalemate though. There was a new smell in the house. I detected it from my place under the bed. I'd never smelled it before, but it was delightful.

"Ruby, I have a nice special dinner for you."

I was still cautious, but now feeling like I was not threatened physically at least. I was also curious as hell about that smell. So I ventured out, slowly, as if I was quietly sizing up a squirrel in the distance. The human had placed the bowl where it was yesterday, but the aroma that beckoned was much more than the dried grotesqueries that had passed for dinner the night before. What could possibly have allowed him to think I'd want to eat the same thing I was forced to live on at the shelter/prison? I wanted nothing to do with anything that reminded me of that place. But oh, this new delicious scent. The human was back at his place on the couch, and like the night before, he wasn't moving a muscle. I looked into the bowl, and saw those same brown nuggets, but there were flecks of light color mixed in as well. They were the same color as the human's skin. I extended my tongue out gently, and flicked one of the pieces into my mouth.

WHERE HAVE YOU BEEN ALL MY LIFE?

Turkey! Oh, I could so wax poetic about how good this meal was. I ate every single nugget simply because some turkey scent was on them.

"Good girl, Ruby."

As soon as I heard him speak, I tore back to my spot under the bed. Later that night, he coerced me into another walk around the cul-de-sac. But I refused to, as he was beseeching me to do, do my "duty." Hate that term, sounds so, I don't know, military. When we got back into the house, the moment he unhooked the leash, I retreated immediately into my crate and slept through the night.

It was mid-afternoon the next day when I overheard him on the phone. "I don't know. She won't come out from under the bed, she hasn't crapped. She must have been beaten really badly. She always looks so scared. I'm trying, but I don't know what more to do. Yeah. Uh huh. No, I haven't tried that. I don't want to scare her any more than she is. I get it. I have to be the Alpha. You think? Okay, anything's worth a try."

After hanging up, I heard him go back into the kitchen, and then advance towards the bedroom. There was the broomstick again, and as he had the first time, he swept it cautiously under the bed, forcing me out. I had not learned my lesson though, and found myself once again, scooped up into his arms. I didn't wriggle around much this time, and he took me over to the couch, sat down, held me with one arm, and I heard the leash clasp to my collar.

"Ruby, you're going to sit here and watch TV with me. Period."

He began to put me down on the floor and I was all ready to make a bee line to my safe place. The moment my paws hit the carpet, I was off, only to find myself yanked unceremoniously, mid-stride, to the ground. My new human had placed the grip of the leash under the leg of the coffee table. I was, effectively, tethered in a place I didn't want to be. I looked back at him, and caught the hint of a shit-eating grin, which left me nothing but more indignant at my plight. OOOhh, big tough human can finally outmaneuver a canine that weights 130 pounds less than you. No wonder you're so proud of yourself.

"Stay, Ruby."

And my other choice?

"Okay, you stay now and I give you a cookie."

He went to the kitchen, and when he did I tugged as much as I could, an action that only confirmed my imprisonment. He came back and sat on the couch. I turned away from him.

"Cookie, Ruby. Here, baby, have this cookie."

He held it out in front of him. What? Did he think I was going to get closer to him than I had to be? That I would be stupid enough to take it from his hand? No. Just throw it on the ground. Go on. I'll eat your damn cookie, just throw it down here.

"Here, Ruby, you have to take it from me."

I was now faced with a moral dilemma. Do I risk taking the cookie from his hand? Risk having him pull it back and hit me? But the cookies are so good. The smell, the texture, the sound they make when I chew them, the way they break up and fall into little pieces that only end up prolonging the epicurean pleasure.

"Come on, baby."

Slowly I turned, inch by inch, step by step. He held the cookie inches above the carpet, all the way at one end so his fingers weren't in imminent danger (proving that I was not the only one with trust issues).

As gently as I could, I opened my mouth and took the very tip of the cookie with my teeth. I could sense him ease up on the pressure with which he was holding his end, and lo and behold, I had the cookie, free and clear, no beating! I swear, that particular cookie may as well have been filet mignon. When I finished it, I could feel my stomach bulging. I knew I was long overdue to, um, go "number two," but my modesty, and maybe my vanity, as well as my lack of trust, wouldn't have it.

I ask you this point blank; name the number of humans in front of whom you would feel comfortable executing a bowel movement?

I rest my case.

> *Heaven goes by favour. If it went by merit, you would stay out and your dog would go in.*
> Mark Twain

CHAPTER TWELVE

ALL DOGS GO TO HEAVEN

There will come a time when my human is going to be forced to make a very tough decision about me. I will be old, I will be infirm. Maybe the very last vestiges of my dignity will have been taken from me and I will not be able to control when and where I relieve myself. Perhaps I'll have some disease that will take advantage of my age-weakened defenses. Whatever the reason, it will happen.

Dog willing, I'm years away from that time. But after the years I've spent with my human, I have faith that he will make the right call. We canines do not have power over this. Only our most feral relatives ever really did. We know the score. The luckiest of us will have the timing of our fates decided by humans who loved us, who lived with us, who know us, who understand what is best for us. Many cannot say that. Too many face "the needle" because they could find no human who cared enough, and by sheer numbers, had to be culled. Some will have the decision made because of their aggressive temperaments towards humans (temperaments bred and trained into them by humans I add, oh the irony).

As a matter of fact, you all seem to have no problem labeling certain breeds of canines as "bad" based on a few isolated incidents, and shuffling them off to the executioner. Years ago, it was the German Shepherd, then the Doberman, the Rottweiler, and now the Pit Bull. I admit some of the attacks have been horrific and I condemn the *individual* canines who committed those crimes. But I'm smart enough not to be prejudiced against every single Pit Bull because of the attack of a lunatic or two. I mean, you humans would never condemn an entire race or religion for the acts of the lunatic fringe or a few misanthropes. right?

You're right, bad example.

Okay, let's play a game real quick. Who do you think has killed more humans, Pit Bulls or humans?

But I mean, to tar an entire race with the same brush because of the perceived behavior of a few is hmmm, let's see, racism? No. Anti-semitism? No. Ageism? No. Could it be *human?*

I report, you decide.

This whole process of euthanasia strikes me as another amazing contrast between us and you. See, with us, you all feel totally qualified to make that final life-or-death decision. In truth, you are! So when you make that decision, don't feel bad, don't feel guilty. We know what's up. We know that you're doing us a favor. Nature granted us the gift of truly living in the moment, so we have a huge advantage over you all; we will feel no sadness. We will, in fact, simply drift off to sleep.

It is you who are left to mourn what was, you left with the memories. A life lacking dignity, lacking self-control, of not being who we really are is not a life we would choose. While I would rather most of you linger on the good times and allow the joy of those times to trump the pain of the loss you're experiencing, I've come to learn that's a part of being human, a good part, a necessary part. The emotion you experience of being here after we're sent to that final sleep is a lot tougher than what we experience.

So let me ask you this. If you know that what you're doing is the right thing, and I know what you're doing is the right thing, even though we canines have zero input into setting the time, date and circumstance of this decision, how come you are all so against other humans making this very same decision about themselves or the humans they love?

In the hierarchy of the world, we canines have grudgingly come to accept that you have the power. Generations tethered to a leash will do that.

OOOOH, LOOK AT THE BIG HUMANS! JUST BECAUSE THEY CAN REASON AND COMMUNICATE IN MULTIPLE SYLLABLES, THEY GET TO RULE THE WORLD. (And after seeing some of your presidential choices, sort of makes me wish the dinosaurs would get one more crack at it.) But that's the way it is.

Now one of your humans gets sick, I mean really sick. The big "C," AIDS, whatever. It's at a stage where the pain is too much, or he's incapacitated completely, beholden totally to others to do the most mundane things life requires. He's intelligent, he's had the chance to figure this all out, and he decides that life is no longer worth living, and he just wants to go to sleep. Please explain to me how it's not MORE right that he has the power to make that decision and then to follow through with it, than to inflict further misery on him? It's okay for you to make that decision for us, but you aren't allowing your fellow humans to make it for themselves? Or for those who can't make it for themselves, by someone who loves them as much as they love themselves?

Sorry people. That doesn't make sense.

The unfortunate truth is, little of what you guys do, does.

There is no psychiatrist in the world like a puppy licking your face.

Ben Williams

CHAPTER THIRTEEN

TRADING PLACES

I'm afraid we're going to have to make a slight change of format as I move forward with this book. Let me explain.

I've had to be very careful about when I can work on it. Thankfully, my current human is very predictable in his day-to-day routine. I can count on him being gone to the gym every morning from 8:30 to 11.

He leaves the computer on during that time (and the radio, in that quaint custom humans have of wanting to keep us somewhat entertained when we are left home alone), so I can get some quality writing time in each morning. When he gets to bed late, there are times when he forgets to shut the computer off, so after he starts snoring, I can usually steal a few more hours here and there. Unfortunately, I haven't the reach to get to the button that turns it on, so my time is limited. But I've never lost sight of the importance of this work, because it may be the only chance we canines have of communicating with you on a level you really understand. So I was always *très* careful to hide my tracks. I even figured out a way to save the manuscript by using a file he'd had on his desktop that was marked by an icon he never used. I had it all figured out.

Or so I thought.

See, this morning when he got back from the gym, his routine was different. Usually, he comes in, tosses his laundry into the hamper, checks his emails, wakes me up (I was always feigning sleep of course, having spent my alone-time wide awake at the computer working on this manuscript), and then gets ready for our noon-time long walkies. Today, the "wakes me up" part was a little different.

"Ruby, I know you're awake."

I thought he was just joking around.

"Ruby, come here."

He was sitting at the computer, not unusual, my thought was that he had more email than usual. When I walked into his office, he gave me the oddest look (and this says something considering how odd he looks on a day-to-day basis) then reached down and picked me up, holding me in his lap.

"Ruby, you have some 'splainin' to do." With that, he turned my chin towards the computer screen.

Busted. He'd found the manuscript.

"Well?"

I'm not sure what he expected to hear from me. I mean, this discovery just proved that I could write the human language, not that I could speak it. I mean come on, let's keep this within the realm of believability.

"Okay, type for me."

So I did. I wrote how I'd been given this unique gift from Dog, and that I wanted to use it to give humans some insight into what it's like to be a canine. What bad could come from that? And what the hell, if I made it to Oprah, I'd insist he get a seat in the audience.

"My computer," he said in a tone that can only be described as cutthroat. "Fifty percent of the royalties."

Ten.

"Thirty-five."

Ten.

"Thirty."

Ten.

"Twenty-five. It's a short car ride back to Indiana."

Sold! To the Greek with the receding hairline. But he had another demand.

"Two chapters."

What?

"Two chapters, so I can tell my side of things."

Fine. But I have final edit. We gave paw on it. So, in the interest of continuity, I'm giving him the rest of this chapter, which will count as one, and two more at the very end. I apologize in advance for his writing style, which I find a bit pedestrian.

Where to begin? I guess I should introduce myself. My name's Tom, and in the previous pages of this book, I'm the one referred to as Ruby's current human. If I had to give you a thumbnail description of my life to date, I would tell you I was born and raised in Chicago (Go Cubs! Go Bears! Go Bulls! Deep Dish Pizza! Oprah!), have spent most of my adult life coaching hockey, have written two books, love Motown in general and Diana Ross in particular, am a dyed in the wool Democrat, and have never been married. (Do the math.)

As I write this I'm fifty-one years old, and I adopted Ruby nearly four years ago. I've always loved dogs, and have been wanting to get one for as long as I can remember. When I was a kid, my younger siblings were allergic to animal hair, and neither of my folks were really dog people. But my paternal grandmother (or Yia Yia in the Greek vernacular), Panayota Adrahtas, loved dogs, as did her daughter Ginny and son-in-law Al, my aunt and uncle. They never had children, but fairly early on in their marriage, as the story goes, my uncle brought up the idea of getting a puppy. My aunt was totally against it, but my uncle convinced her to give it a try. If she didn't like the experience of having a dog at home, they would return it to the breeder. Now when my uncle wanted to bring a dog home, he really meant it. He wasn't talking about a poodle, or some God-awful teacup something or other (and as far as I'm concerned, those Paris Hilton accessory breeds are nothing but cats with bad extensions), he was talking a real dog.

Can you say, "Great Dane?" Yes, he went out and brought home a fawn Great Dane puppy. And my aunt? The dog was in the house for all of three days before she had a question for my uncle.

"Can we get another one?" And they did.

My first memories of visiting my aunt and uncle's house as a child were of those enormous, majestic, loving creatures. They never intimidated me one bit. I recall that time whenever I walk Ruby. When we walk past little children, their first reaction is always to smile widely and come towards her. The natural human instinctive relationship between man and dog is one of trust. Like prejudice, fear is a learned behavior.

Yia Yia lived with my aunt and uncle, and while they both worked long hours, she was in charge of the Danes during the day. That made for an interesting juxtaposition. The Danes, Duchess and Lady, were both fawn, sleek and long-legged.

My grandmother, on the other hand, was a typical Greek Yia Yia.

Four foot eleven. Two hundred and fifty pounds. Moustache. Her hair was thin and wispy, and she walked with a gentle waddle.

The only thing better than getting a Yia Yia hug was seeing her hug those dogs. She'd wrap her thick, fleshy arms around them and coo sweet nothings, and in turn they'd cover her with sloppy kisses that would knock her glasses askew. Lady would back up towards Yia Yia when she was sitting on the couch, bend her back legs and dip her butt onto Yia Yia's knees, and there she'd sit as they both watched TV. Duchess would see this and make her way to the couch and sit next to the pair, all three focused on the screen.

When it was time for them to "go," Yia Yia would hitch up their leashes, hand one to me (usually Duchess's), and out to the yard we went. My aunt's yard was always a source of pride for her and my uncle, an elaborately decorated rock garden sprinkled with deliberately placed pagodas and smiling Buddhas. On the side of the house grew a peach tree and two olive trees, planted and tended to by Yia Yia. Beyond that stretched a large lawn, where the Danes could run. I gripped Duchess's leash and we'd run up and down along the side of the house. I felt like I was training a Temple Lippizan.

We'd return to the house after a time, and the dogs would be exhausted, slurping happily at the great silver bowls of water that Yia Yia had ready and waiting, then both would climb up on a couch in the den and fall fast asleep. This was one of my favorite times as a child. I would sit on the floor, and Yia Yia would massage my shoulders with her worn hands that still had the strength of her Olympian forebears, and convey her special brand of wisdom. The world had not been especially kind to her throughout her life. She fled Greece as a young teen, escaping the invading Turks to come to America and the hope of a better life.

Her education was limited. The necessity of working the fields in the old country meant that she'd get no farther than the second grade, and when she married in the new country, her husband basically left her alone to raise four children, walking out the door one day and never coming back.

Despite the adversity, she never lost her sense of humor, her timeless laugh, or an innate sense of wisdom that left her with the world's perfect bullshit detector. Anyone in her presence who tried to exude any false airs would quickly be confronted with rolling eyes and an impatient turn of her lip. Those gestures said more than any words could have, and had the same effect as piercing a balloon with a needle. She had a way of cutting to the chase about any situation, her halting, thickly accented English making our conversations all the more memorable.

I had a difficult relationship with my father, who happened to be her son. When she saw how affected I was by one of our increasingly regular rows, she sidled up next to me, enveloped me in her arms and said, "Tommy, I try keel heem when he was leettle but he kept getting away."

I saw my aunt and uncle's house as a sanctuary. It was where I could spend time with Yia Yia, and where I could lose myself in the love of those Danes. And of course, Yia Yia imparted never-to-be-forgotten wisdom about those four-legged companions. I was sure that she was thinking about her long-gone husband, and perhaps another relative or two who'd managed to disappoint her along the way when she shared this nugget with me.

"Tommy, is to always remember this. The dogs is better than the pipples."

And of course, truer words were never spoken.

🐾   🐾   🐾

I traveled a lot with my work over the years, never with enough stay-at-home interval to make a good home for a dog. But I don't think more than two or three days ever passed without thinking about how badly I wanted one. The door finally opened for me when the stress of my job mandated that I take a step back. I got off the coaching merry-go-round and into work where I was overseeing a youth hockey organization and traveling only very occasionally. No sooner had I settled into this job than I began looking. When I started the process, I knew exactly what I wanted; I was going to adopt a Greyhound. I saw them as sort of Great Dane lites. Not as big as Danes, which was important for me as a condo resident, they were similarly long-legged, majestic in their bearing, and I'd read that there was a great need for them to be adopted when their racing careers were over. They were sedate in temperament as well, wanting to be little more than couch potatoes once people lost interest in betting on their speed. I did all the research, put in the applications, and found myself frustrated because the adoption waiting period was so long.

So I began scouring shelters in the Chicago area. I knew I wanted to adopt from a shelter because I knew that was the right thing to do. I wanted to save a dog, give it the love I never felt I'd gotten enough of, and in return have a companion that was "better than the pipples."

I looked at hundreds of dogs, young, old, big, medium. I fell in love with nearly all of them. But I kept hesitating, kept finding some reason to put off a final decision. Oddly enough, I was driving home from visiting my aunt one day (she lived alone in the same house as the one I'd visited as a kid; Yia Yia had been gone thirteen years already before we lost my uncle) when I stopped at a dinky little shelter that had not impressed me much the first time I'd dropped in. I thought it was dank and spare, the workers a bit too unorganized, the whole environment a tad depressing. I only stopped in again because I had a few moments to kill before going in to work.

The place looked like a converted home, with a long rectangular room off the office area that held about fourteen chain link kennels. I signed in and took a quick stroll around the area. I didn't feel any strong connection with any of the dogs, but wasn't disappointed because I didn't expect to. My first time here, I hadn't noticed that there was another row of kennels in sort of a back room area, so I peeked in, and that's when I saw Ruby for the first time.

She was a terrified, trembling, chunky little thing. She had crushed herself into the back of her kennel, only occasionally turning back to look at me, and almost as soon as our eyes met, she turned away and tucked her head into her chest, I assume taking solace in the comfort of the fetal position. I knelt down and tried to get a better look at her. She was having none of me. But I kept looking anyway. She was a beautiful girl, the perfect mix between a Beagle and a Terrier, with tri-color Beagle coloring and a Terrier face. What struck me immediately was that I didn't think I'd ever seen another living creature that looked so utterly alone. I could identify.

There was an information card attached to the top of the kennel.

NAME: RUBY
BREED: BEAGLE MIX
SEX: F SPAYED: NO
AGE: 1.5 YRS.
SHOTS: YES
TEMPERAMENT: UNDETERMINED

I walked back to the office area and asked one of the attendants if she knew anything about her, and if I could see her outside her kennel. The attendant gave me the background story about the Indiana state trooper and all, and frankly at first I thought it was a story concocted to evoke pity from any prospective adopter. No matter, she walked back towards the kennel, and told me to wait in the common room. I sat on a threadbare couch, some remnant of a badly furnished apartment circa 1963. Moments later, the attendant led Ruby through the door, unhooked her leash and let her go. With the manic stride of a speed walker, Ruby inspected everything in the room, except me. She sniffed at the corners, sniffed near the door, and sniffed under the couch. She kept moving as if her life depended on it.

"Hey Ruby, come up here." I swatted the couch, beckoning for her to hop up. That was the only time we made eye contact, and she threw me the very same look Yia Yia used to aim at a bullshitter. So I slipped off the couch and went prone on the floor. This little gambit got her attention, but it was several minutes before she showed any overt curiosity. Even then, she still kept her distance. She looked puzzled, but for the first time, made longer than cursory eye contact. She had the most beautiful brown eyes, alert, but far too naturally sad for a dog her age.

She crept up closer, and came within inches of my nose. I sensed that this was an act of immense trust on her part, and took care not to move a muscle. I could feel her breath against my face. I said nothing. She took another half step, and almost imperceptibly, she darted her tongue out, making contact with my nose, and then immediately stepped back.

That was it. This was going to be my dog.

And I was going to be her human.

> *Recollect that the Almighty, who gave the dog to be companion of our pleasures and our toils, hath invested him with a nature noble and incapable of deceit.*
> Sir Walter Scott

CHAPTER FOURTEEN

YOUR ONE-MINUTE CANINE-CENTRIC MOVIE REVIEWS, *OR* I CAN DO MORE WITH ONE PAW THAN ROGER EBERT CAN DO WITH TWO THUMBS

Since we canines do more than our share of TV watching, I thought I'd give you a peek into exactly how we see the movies you watch. So here are my reviews of some of the more popular fare out there. The movies are rated on a scale of one to four dead cats, four being the best possible grade.

DOG DAY AFTERNOON

Bisexual Al Pacino loves Fredo and robs a bank. Producer should have been sued for false advertising. There's not a canine in the entire movie.

RUBY'S RATING: No rating

OLD YELLER

How do you get a theater full of humans to cry at the same time? No, you don't announce that Springsteen can't perform tonight, so the Osmond Family will take the stage in his stead. You make them watch this flick.

RUBY'S RATING: Superlative! 4 dead cats

LASSIE, LASSIE COME HOME, LASSIE RETURNS, LASSIE MEETS THE WOLFMAN, LASSIE TAKES MANHATTAN, ETC.

Proof positive of a great idea gone down the toilet because of too many sequels. The last one was as bad as Rocky Whatever The Last Number Was. Give Lassie all the credit, though, to pull off such a convincing role in drag hasn't been done since Liza in Cabaret.

RUBY'S RATING: 3.5 dead cats for the original, one dead cat each for the sequels

SILENCE OF THE LAMBS

Yeah yeah, Hopkins was great, Foster was great. But the pivotal character was Precious. Without her, the senator's daughter ends up on a hanger.

RUBY'S RATING: 4 dead cats

101 DALMATIONS

The animated version is THE version. Glenn Close was in the remake of course. She's been a favorite of mine ever since she boiled that rabbit.

RUBY'S RATING: 2.5 dead cats

LADY AND THE TRAMP

A love story for the entire litter.

RUBYS'S RATING: 4 dead cats

THE UGLY DACHSHUND

As if dachshunds couldn't tell their own kind from a Great Dane. Oh, the titles they could get away with before the era of political correctness.

RUBY'S RATING:1.5 dead cats

BENJI

Cute enough, but hardly profound. For you history buffs, the Benji character sprang from the insipid 60s sitcom, *Petticoat Junction,* which was sort of a spin-off from *The Beverly Hillbillies* which featured that pitiful bloodhound of Jedd Clampett's. It should be noted that the bloodhound, while an offensive and rank stereotype of slobbering slovenliness, was demonstrably brighter than Jethro.

RUBY'S RATING: 2 dead cats

UNDERDOG

Another film that failed to live up to the original cartoon. While I was personally complimented that the producers opted for a Beagle in the live-action version as opposed to the unidentifiable (if well-intentioned) breed in the cartoon, I still must recognize that it bombed at the box office, deservedly.

RUBY'S RATING: 1 dead cat

BEACHES

A real tear jerker. I mean, there wasn't a dry eye in the house when Bette Midler revealed that the Great Dane had been hit by a car.

RUBY'S RATING: 3 dead cats

STRAW DOGS

(See Dog Day Afternoon, *sans* the alternate lifestyle issues.)

RUBY'S RATING: no rating

EIGHT BELOW

Canines brave the odds against Mother Nature, show amazing courage, and get to spend quality time with Paul Walker!

RUBY'S RATING: 3 dead cats

SNOW DOGS

Canines brave the odds against Mother Nature, and show amazing courage by spending quality time with Cuba Gooding Jr.

RUBY'S RATING: half a dead cat—the back half.

THERE'S SOMETHING ABOUT MARY

This has all the appeal of a snuff film. What that poor canine went through to satisfy some demented twenty-year-old human's idea of humor. Where in the hell was the SPCA?

RUBY'S RATING: zero dead cats

FERRIS BUELLER'S DAY OFF

Who will ever forget the triumph of the canine over the vile guidance counselor?

RUBY'S RATING: 3 dead cats

CUJO

Could have been a classic, except for the ending. Why do you humans always kill what you don't understand? Cujo just needed a little love.

RUBY'S RATING: 3 dead cats

THE OMEN

Finally, a good guy wins.

RUBY'S RATING: 3.5 dead cats

THE HOUND OF THE BASKERVILLES

The old classic version with Basil Rathbone, but my favorite is the one with Peter Cushing and Christopher Lee. In that one, the title hound is a Great Dane wearing a papier-mâché mask. Some mystery, Sherlock.

RUBY'S RATING: 1 dead cat

AIR BUD

There's a certain segment of the human population who think this movie is about smoking weed in a plane.

RUBY'S RATING: 2 dead cats.

TURNER AND HOOCH

See Tom Hanks before he was Tom Hanks. To be kind, Hooch clearly suffered from poor direction.

RUBY'S RATING: 1 dead cat

STAND BY ME

There are classic movie lines, and there are classic movie lines. "Frankly my dear ... Rosebud ... Play it Sam ... I think we're going to need a bigger boat ... Senator, love your suit ... I'm mad as hell, and I'm not going to take it anymore." But none of them compare with, "Chopper, sic balls."

RUBY'S RATING: 4 dead cats.

THE TRUTH ABOUT CATS AND DOGS

You can't handle the truth.

RUBY'S RATING: 2 dead cats.

DOWN AND OUT IN BEVERLY HILLS

In the end, it was all about Matisse.

RUBY'S RATING: 3 dead cats.

THE WIZARD OF OZ

Tragically, this was Toto's last movie. As is well known, he couldn't handle the fame, and his life spiraled out of control. He died penniless in a fleabag hotel. His last words? "Auntie Em was a whore!"

RUBY'S RATING: 4 dead cats

BEST IN SHOW

The movie that is the *Citizen Kane* of the canine cinema.

RUBY'S RATING: 5, yes 5 dead cats

> *When a man's best friend is his dog,*
> *that dog has a problem.*
> Edward Abbey

CHAPTER FIFTEEN

SLEEPER

As high as my level of distrust was, my current human *was* going the extra mile. Ever so slowly, he was chipping away at my defenses. After only a few days, I did not need to be coerced to stay in the same room as he. Around the same time, the combination of my growing trust, final acceptance that we did not have a yard, and at-full-capacity lower intestine dictated that I would have my first bowel movement since the adoption. I did so while out on one of our walkies, to my current human's almost eerily joyous delight.

"Good girl, Ruby! Oh, I'm so proud of my girl. You're the best girl in the whole world. Oh, what a good doggie."

Mortifying, I tell you.

Another rather pedestrian action of mine that seemed to engender a state of ecstasy from him was when I took a nap in the "doggy bed" he'd bought. See, when you're in a new house like I was, the safe thing to do is to sleep where you have some protection, so all of my naps or overnights had taken place in my crate. He had placed this wonderful, perfectly-sized doggy bed near the crate, but it left me too exposed. It was maybe the fifth day I was there before I decided to give it a whirl, intending only to test it out. Before I knew it, I was snoring. When I woke up, there he was, staring, a big dumb grin on his face. It was endearing in a creepy sort of stalkerish kind of way. As it happened, it was the very next day that I had my first furniture breakthrough.

It was early afternoon, and we'd just gotten back from our long walkie. There'd been a little snow on the ground as I recall, and when we got back in the house, he took great care to wipe the moisture from my paws. Now I don't particularly like my paws messed with, but things had been going well so I didn't make a fuss. It was up the stairs, have a treat, and usually time for the crate and a little nap. But he didn't unleash me, and instead of going to his office, he went and sat on the couch.

That big, luscious, inviting, forbidden couch.

"Ruby. Come on up here. I want you to sit with me." And like he had the day I met him at the shelter, he patted his hand hard on the couch's surface. I looked at him, and I knew that he knew that I knew what he knew. I'd been beaten previously for jumping on the couch.

"It's okay, girl. I want you to be up here with me."

I sat, staring, transfixed. This was going to be the crossroad, right here. If I jump up there and he hits me, I would be back to square one and I would have to plot my escape. And a jailbreak from a gardenless condo was a whole different animal (you should excuse the pun) than slipping under a fence. This would mean playing Houdini from my collar while we were out for a walkie. Once I was loose, I could outrun anyone.

That would be the easy part. But getting loose?

"Ruby."

I snapped back into the moment. Dare I jump up there? Everything was riding on this. Slowly, I stood.

"Come on, baby." I took one step forward. It was now or never.

I jumped.

"Good girl! Oh, that's a good girl."

I tensed, expecting the swat.

Nothing. Nothing but praise.

"Good girl, Ruby! Oh, that's my good girl. Oh, I'm so proud of you!"

So to recap, within a space of forty-eight hours, I'd earned praise befitting a Nobel Prize winner for taking a crap and jumping up on a couch. And you thought affirmative action set the bar low.

Once on the couch, I sat within a foot of him, my back to him. I felt his hand caressing my back. It was nice. Almost like what I'd heard this canine-to-human interaction was supposed to be like. He kept petting, kept talking in a near whisper about how I was his good girl, and I didn't have to be afraid anymore. It was sweet. Maybe, just maybe, he was for real. I turned and looked at him.

"You are such a pretty girl. How could anyone have ever hit you?"

I don't know. I really don't. But please, please, don't you hit me, okay? It would break my heart.

🐾 🐾 🐾

Having broken the furniture ceiling, the next wall that came tumbling down would occur at "seepie-time."

Yes, can you believe it? "Seepie-time" was bedtime. *Seepie* time. And this guy's a hockey coach. I think it was the second week home when one night I noticed that the door to my crate was closed and bolted. My human was already in bed, so I went to lie down in the doggy bed, and that was gone too.

"Ruby, your bed's up here. Come on girl, seepie time."

And there, indeed, was my bed. It was on his bed, inches from his feet. The access I'd been granted to the couch made this a far less daunting challenge, so I jumped up, walked around the bed at first, pawed at the covers for a second and stepped into the doggy bed. The shape of my bed basically made the fetal position my only sleeping option. I think the expression you humans use when you don't particularly trust someone is that you "sleep with one eye open." That fits what I was feeling perfectly. I decided to keep that one eye on him, refusing to nod off completely until I heard his telltale snores. As it turned out, this was going to be some battle of wills, because he'd propped up his head on an extra pillow, and was staring right back at me. What, did he think I was a cat and was going to suck the breath out of him once he went "seepie-time?"

(And while I know many of you think that's an urban legend, I'm here to tell you that it's a known and accepted medical fact in the greater canine community that cats do, in fact, suck the breath out of sleeping humans every opportunity they get. I bet you didn't know that John Wilkes Booth had a cat. And so did the JFK conspirators. Coincidence? I think not.)

We stayed like that for quite some time, but I'm happy to report that it was my current human who succumbed to the wiles of Morpheus first. I eventually drifted off into a fitful sleep, awakened at about three AM when my current human had to make a trip to the washroom. It was one thing to be "allowed" to sleep in the human bed, but it felt a lot less privileged if that meant that I couldn't sleep the whole night through because his kidneys were weaker than mine. When he crawled back into bed, he looked over at me and said, "Good girl, Ruby. Go back seepy."

I groaned, and tucked my head down, wishing for a recurrence of my favorite dream, the one, where I live in a world of quadriplegic rabbits and morbidly obese squirrels.

I woke before my human, nature urgently begging me to go outside. What to do? I looked over at him, and it was, frankly, an appalling sight. He was asleep on his stomach, legs askew under the comforter (and I give him this; he had great taste in bedding: it was Nate Berkus or nothing), head turned to its left, mouth gaping and trailing a fine line of spittle, the noises being emitted through his nose more likely to be heard from a hyena giving birth. If I moved around enough, maybe I'd wake him. I took a shot, walked in a little circle, pawed at the covers. Nothing.

Okay, time to take it to the next level. I jumped down, walked to the side of the bed and stared at him.

Still nothing. So I jumped back up on the bed, hoping the vibrations would do the trick. He remained comatose, the only sign of life being the noise made by the hollow wail of wind wafting through his nostrils. All this time, the need for me to commune with the green green grass outside of the home grew more dire. I took a few cautious steps alongside his prone body until I was inches from his left hand. We were entering Emergency Code Red territory now, so I dipped my nose and pushed his hand. His fingers moved reflexively. Okay, progress. I pushed again, and he moved his entire arm.

"Good morning, girl," he wheezed, the blast of his abhorrent morning-breath bringing tears to my eyes.

Mercifully, he turned his head to the right, and I was able to recoup my senses against the onslaught of the stench. Folks, trust me, someone finds a way to bottle that stink, all we have to do is drop a little in mountainous Afghanistan and Osama will come a-runnin'.

He still wasn't moving very much, so I kept moving. I began thrusting my nose into his arm, pushing it closer to the headboard. He moved a little more, but he wasn't showing anywhere near the urgency I needed. So it was time for an assault on his torso. With his arm extended up, his ribs were an inviting target.

I sent my nose into them, followed quickly by my paw.

"Aw Ruby! That's so cute. You want me to get up?"

Cute? Cute? YES, I WANT YOU TO GET UP. Exactly how cute do you think it will be if I pee all over your comfortable bedding? You're the genius who bought a canine without having a yard and a doggy door.

Lucky for you if I do let go in the bed, the smell won't be any worse than that skunk bait you call breath. So with my kidneys backed up to the point where my teeth were turning yellow, I was moved to my absolute desperate lowest.

I barked. Yes, dear reader, for the first time since he'd brought me home from the shelter, he heard my canine voice.

"Ruby! Oh, so you do bark. I guess you're trying to tell me something."

WAY TO GO EINSTEIN, NOW GET YOUR LAZY ASS UP AND TAKE ME OUTSIDE BEFORE I TURN YOUR KING SIZED BED INTO A KIDDIE POOL.

That morning pretty much set the routine we've developed from then on. One could contend that I'd been reduced to the role of being little more than a thirty-five-pound, fur-covered alarm clock. I preferred to see myself as the day's agenda-setter.

> *I've seen a look in dogs' eyes, a quickly vanishing look of amazed contempt, and I am convinced that basically dogs think humans are nuts.*
> John Steinbeck

CHAPTER SIXTEEN

RUBY'S TV GUIDE

Television often gets short shrift when it comes to prestige. The Emmys are wonderful, but they're not quite the Oscars, or so goes conventional wisdom. That's a human-defined bias, so let me wax poetic about some inspirational canines and humans whose work on the small screen and in the newspapers has left an indelible (sometimes positive, sometimes negative) paw print on popular culture.

EDDIE

As a Beagle-Terrier mix, I can testify directly as to what a role model and inspiration this star of *Frasier* was. He may not have had the same face time as Kelsey Grammar, but when they were both on the screen, there was only one you were looking at. And that, my friends, is the true measure of a star.

LASSIE

This was the first canine to have a series of his/her own. Thank you for paving the way, and being such a role model to the transgender community besides.

TRIUMPH, THE INSULT DOG

Says everything we'd all like to say, and humps many we'd all like to hump. (Don't deny it.)

BETTY WHITE

See above.

BOB BARKER

The pied piper of planned parenthood.

KATHY GRIFFIN

You're an "A" lister in my book (which this is) if you love canines as much as she does. Who else would go on national television and don a squirrel suit in an attempt to help train those canines (who were better to her than her rat bastard of en ex-husband).

SNOOPY

The world's most famous Beagle, and the rare crossover artists who made the successful transition from newspaper to television.

FRED BASSETT

Has there ever been one human being who laughed at this comic?

MARMADUKE

We get it; it's funny because he's so big. Ugh.

SCOOBY DOO

Renough rith rhe Reat Ranes ralready!

BANDIT

This was the dog on *Little House on the Prairie*. Don't

remember? That's to your credit.

BLUE

Blue's clues helped educate a generation. How frightening is that?

COMET

This was the dog on *Full House*. (See Bandit.)

AUGIE DOGGY AND DADDY DOGGIE

This was an old-school Hanna-Barberra style cartoon. Funny in a 60s lame sitcom sort of way.

PRECIOUS PUP

Speaking of old-school Hanna Barbera, this character had the best laugh in the history of animation.

FLEAGLE

Speaking of the 60s, how about someone selling network TV executives on the idea of a human in a bad, enormous beagle costume prancing around on the Saturday morning hit, *The Banana Splits*. There has never been a more convincing testimony for "Say no to drugs.'

TRAMP

May as well stay in the 60s and mention the Sheepdog on *My Three Sons*. I always wondered what Uncle Charley's real story was. Don't you think he was just a little too fond of wearing that apron?

SPANKY

Speaking of Uncle Charley, this is Stan's gay dog in *South Park*. We do well to remember that this breakthrough character came onto the national scene well before *Brokeback Mountain*.

DREYFUSS

The dog on *Empty Nest*. (See Comet, and then see Bandit.)

McGRUFF

The anti-crime dog bit sure has been effective, huh.

RIN TIN TIN

Now THAT was a dog.

GARY LARSEN AND THE FAR SIDE

The world is poorer for the fact that he does not grace us with his genius anymore. His depiction of the dog world was more portrait than caricature, and *The Far Side* was the one moment in your day that you knew you were going to laugh.

> *To his dog, every man is Napoleon,*
> *hence the popularity of dogs.*
> Aldous Huxley

CHAPTER SEVENTEEN

TORN BETWEEN TWO LOVERS

Six weeks passed, and my current human and I began to settle into a comfortable routine. During this time, I had come to accept my fate of living in a home without a garden, the acceptable trade-off being that my human had been almost unfailingly good to me. Forgive the repetition as I state again that my past experiences made opening my heart to any human nearly unfathomable. But this back-half-of-middle-aged (in human years), balding, single, large-nosed Homo sapiens of Greek descent had really worn my resistance down. I was receiving a lot of love from him in words and deed, and I'd nearly been pushed to the point of feeling like I owed him some of that same emotion in return. Nearly.

But there were still a few hiccups to occur in our relationship.

Just three weeks into my stay, my current human told me we were going for a ride. I've detailed earlier my weakness for that word, my enjoyment of speeding along in an automobile enjoying the passing vista and the torrent of scents that whip their way through an open window and bombard my senses. So little did I realize that this particular ride was going to end at the building next to the shelter where my current human had adopted me, a building that was an "animal hospital." (This is a good time to share how much that particular designation bothers us canines. Is it asking too much to be a little more specific? "Animal hospital" implies that even humans might be treated there. With the staph infections and other filth your species both attract and spew, labeling these places as such makes a traumatic experience for us all that much worse.)

Was I ill? No. I was the picture of health. I'd never once so much as puked in his home, despite the fact I'd seen him naked on two separate occasions. I'd dropped my pregnancy pounds, I was strong, I was invincible, I was—woman. You get the picture. So what prompted this excursion? My current human had agreed to have me neutered (vets and their ilk prefer "spayed" to neutered, as if a softer-sounding word makes the practice less barbaric) as a pre-condition of my adoption.

I was not amused.

We canines are socially aware enough to know that we have not exactly been responsible when it comes to procreation. We've had too many males impregnate our females and then run off with no thought to the consequences. Just like many of your professional athletes. But unlike them, we can admit responsibility for our role in the population explosion. That doesn't make you humans any less guilty of Big Brother behavior on the grandest of scales. Unlike your pro athletes, we do not have other forms of birth control available to us. How about some of you rocket scientists out there coming up with a canine condom? A doggie diaphragm. A Terrier Trojan. A Rottweiler Rubber.

But apparently, that level of creativity is too much to ask for. So instead, you proceed with the assumption that even given the choice, we wouldn't be responsible. So it's a snip-snip here and a snip-snip there, and you humans get the duel benefit of canine population control and a pet whose personality is more sedate. Need I point out this was the same logic you all employed when lobotomy was all the rage?

So there I was, handed over by my human, who voted Pro-Choice but was acting as a proponent of No Choice, to a vet staff who would perform the surgery. I remember little of that day, but I do remember the ride back home a day or two later. My human was acting especially solicitous of me, trying to curry favor, making professions of how much he missed me and loved me. But I felt betrayed.

We were back to Square One.

Over the next two weeks, he was clearly racked with guilt. Not being heartless, I began to soften, but I must admit to milking it as much as I could. Every so often, I'd let out a little groan to make sure he knew I was feeling some discomfort. This mournful noise elicited a cookie from him every time, and in a funny sort of way, I felt that his reaction was benefiting more than just little old Ruby.

Somewhere in canine heaven, I knew that Pavlov's dog was smiling.

Once I was fully healed, my next goal was to increase the scope of our walkies. During my first month at my new home, we seldom ventured any farther than two times around the cul-de-sac. I needed more, I needed to see more of the world I had been thrust into. I wanted the stimulation of more exercise, wanted the old endorphin rush that I could feel when I tore around my first human's yard. I was able to get that message across with an effective combination of cunning and guile.

My current human returned home from his morning time at

the gym every day at eleven sharp. I had taken to greeting him at the top of the stairs, tail wagging, not so much at being glad to see him as for knowing that I was going to be taken outside for our late-morning twice-around-the cul-de-sac routine that served as one of our long walkies. It was a Wednesday I think, and I heard the car pull into the driveway, heard the garage door open, heard the telltale sound of the key turning. Instead of bounding joyfully to my usual position at the top of the stairs, I simply stayed where I'd been waiting, scrunched comfortably on the edge of his bed.

"Hey, girl, why didn't you come say hello to me?"

Why indeed.

"Come on, let's go for long walkies."

No, I'm pretty comfortable right here. I'll let you know when I want to go outside. (Just to make sure I had him where I wanted him, every so often I'd throw in a pained groan, prompting him to bring me a cookie.)

"Ruby, what's a matter? Come on, baby, you need to go outside."

Slowly, I began to rise, my pace deliberate as I hopped off the bed and sauntered across the condo and down the stairs before sitting near the door and allowing him to attach the leash to my collar.

"That's better."

Not yet it's not. We'd make our first pass around the cul-de-sac, but instead of meekly beginning lap two, I pulled towards the street that lay ahead.

"No Ruby, we're going long walkies."

No "we" aren't. So instead of following him, once he decreed that the regular routine was going to be followed again this day, instead of walking past our home, I made a beeline towards the stairs. I was going on strike.

"Ruby, what are you doing? You wanna go home? Well, okay, we go home then."

I kept it up for a week, every day making him work harder and harder to get me outside. I moped around the house, looking as depressed as I could. I ate less, demanded fewer cookies. It was my homage to Gandhi; I was going to effect change through non-violent revolution.

It took a while but it finally prompted him to call the vet (the same charlatan who had dispensed of my ovaries). It seems the good doctor prescribed more exercise, that a canine of my background was a scent hound, used to the outdoors, used to long runs, in need of the stimulation of sights and smells that were not accessible in a human home. I needed the great outdoors, grasses and trees, squirrels and rabbit shit, meeting other dogs, hearing other noises.

No sooner had my human hung up the phone than he put that sage advice into practice. And not long after that, I became a felon.

My temperament, not surprisingly, became more upbeat in direct proportion to the duration and distance of our walkies. It was early April, unseasonably balmy, and now twice a day we would walk nearly a mile. This new routine had the added benefit of toning my underused muscles. I was looking pretty hot if I say so myself. That hotness brought with it some much-needed attraction from the opposite sex. There were two males in particular whose attentions I was beginning to receive. Both were big, strong and black—just how I liked 'em.

Foster is an Australian Shepherd. He was three years old when we met, a very good age for a gal like me. He had long thick hair, with just the right amount of white on his face and a touch of brown bordering his eyes.

So handsome he was pretty, Foster could have been a show dog had his human so chosen. He was the one my mother would have wanted me to marry. Dotes on me, is respectful, a little playful, well mannered and a worker. His human is a pleasant lady, always smiling, always glad to see me. That goes a long way. Or it should.

But then there was Freddy.

Freddy's a Rottweiler. Thick at nearly one hundred pounds and black as coal, he was a year old when we met. Yes, I found myself interested in a younger male, dangerous, a bad boy. His human was a large man who spoke with a thick Russian accent, and when he crossed paths with my human, I always got the impression he was being just pleasant enough to blend into the neighborhood out of a sense of social obligation, but found being neighborly as distasteful as chewing glass.

Whenever I crossed paths with Foster, he laughed, peed and slobbered. When I crossed paths with Freddy, he was happy enough, but restrained. With both of them I sniffed the requisite sniffs in the requisite areas, and if I'd had a brain in my head I would have simply followed what I learned from those smells and committed to Foster. But that bad-boy allure prevented me from heeding common scents and doing the right thing. I needed Foster, but I wanted Freddy. To make matters more complicated, Foster and Freddy hated each other. H-A-T-

E-D. Their humans would have to stay on opposite sides of the street when they were out at the same time.

Was I being too presumptuous to assume that the root of their problem was their interest in little old me?

Without telling either, I saw them both. My human was savvy enough to know that one of my two daily long walkies happened to coincide with Foster's, the other with Freddy's. So for many months, each morning I would see Foster, exchange pleasantries, flirt just enough to make sure I still had him where I wanted him, and move on. In the afternoons, it was Freddy's turn. I always had to work a little harder to gain his undivided attention, but I usually succeeded. Truth be told, I know a part of my attraction to Freddy was his resemblance to Ralph. They were both the strong silent types. Foster was by far more socially acceptable.

But in matters of the heart, logic does not play even a cameo role.

I realized that it was totally unfair to lead them both on, although I'd be lying if I told you that I didn't enjoy the quandary I was facing. My mind screamed "Foster" but my heart cried for Freddy. In the end, I was going to follow my heart. My lack of romantic experience showed in my choice, however, and in my naïveté I had "the talk" with Foster first. Appropriately, it was a drizzly morning as I recall. During rainy walks, we seldom had a lot of time to spend together, which I hoped would make it less painful for him, the dear heart.

"Foster, I want you to know how much our time together has meant to me. But I'm afraid we can only be friends. You're a terrific guy. You're always well groomed, and you can hold up your end of the conversation. See, it's not you, it's me. I'm not ready to settle down quite yet, and you are a bit older than me. You deserve someone who'll be able to give you more than I'm ready to. But I promise, you need anything, you know I'll be right there for you."

He skewed his head slightly to the left, and I clearly saw him choking back tears. But he was strong in the face of adversity. He turned away, peed a little bit of a good bye, and walked off into the distance with his human.

Now, I was ready to commit to Freddy.

That afternoon, I was especially keyed up for my long walkie. I'd spent the day rehearsing what I was going to say. I wasn't going to make it seem to him like I was just going to lose it and rush into his paws. I knew he wouldn't be the type to respond to that. I had to be a bit more mysterious, a bit harder to get, so I was going to make myself just aloof enough, just that little bit out of his reach to make me all the more tantalizing. When I heard my human tell me that it was time for our long walkie, I raced down the stairs and sat nervously as he affixed the leash to my collar. We usually saw Freddy within minutes of starting our walkie. I was already straining against the leash when my human opened the door. A minute passed, then five. No Freddy. We walked the entire thirty minutes and did not see him anywhere. The same thing happened the next day and the day after that. I knew he lived down the block from us, and successfully changed the route of our walkie to pass by his home. There was a car in the driveway, and I hopped up on the back bumper. His scent was there. But where was he?

A week passed, and still no Freddy.

Then, one morning when my human was talking with Foster's human, as he and I exchanged stilted, uncomfortable small talk, I overheard the answer to the mystery. It seemed that Freddy's human was fond of allowing Freddy off-leash during some of their walkies. Thought it was good for Freddy to prove his obedience to voice commands. Well apparently Freddy's human's voice was no match for a semi-trailer truck that my bad boy decided to race.

It was a fatal decision.

The depression that set in lasted a few weeks, but I was able to move on. Things got more comfortable when I crossed paths with Foster, though I always thought of him more like a brother than anything else.

My current human and I had settled into a nice routine, and as the weather improved from Spring to Summer, we expanded the boundaries of our walkies. It happened that during our first summer together, there was damn near a rabbit infestation in our sub-division. That always made our walkies more adventurous than my human bargained for. It was then that he learned the hard way exactly how vigilant he needed to be about gripping my leash if he expected to keep me within his sights.

That memorable lesson began when we were turning the corner to head for home at the end of one of our walkies. There's a stately pine tree about half a block from our home, and in a flash a bunny, who must have sensed my approach, darted out from under it and tore across the street. At that very instant, my human was transferring my leash from his right hand to his left. The moment that rabbit crossed my path, I was off, tearing the leash from my human's hands in the process. I sped across the street that was mercifully free of traffic, the rabbit my singular focus. I heard my human screaming my name, I sensed him running after me, but the primordial instinct to chase kept driving me towards my prey. The rabbit kept running, as did I, as did my human. Needless to say, the rabbit and I were significantly faster. The only reason my human was able to catch up, was the rabbit's decision to venture into a fenced yard. As it ran, sod flew everywhere. I saw the fence ahead, my mind exploding with the possibilities! Trapped!!!

He's trapped! I'm going to get my first kill! But alas, as I had been robbed of romance with my dear departed Freddy, I was also robbed of victory in my pursuit of the hare. A gap in the fence proved just big enough for the accursed long-eared fur-ball to slip through. By the time I reached the fence, all I saw was a white tail bobbing in the distance.

That white tail. That vision would hound (no pun intended) me. I became obsessed. My sleep became fitful, my dreams racked with the image of that white tail bouncing away, always just out of my reach. This humiliation would prove only temporary. No matter what it took, no matter how long, I would catch that rabbit. Yes, dear readers, I vowed not to rest until I had my murderous revenge on that Great White Tail.

No one appreciates the very special genius
of your conversation as the dog does.
Christopher Marley

CHAPTER EIGHTEEN

THE CONVERSATION

To illustrate just how much you humans have come to rely on us, I thought I'd share some actual conversations that you've had with your canines. How'd I hear about them? You'd be amazed what you can learn if you hang around a dog park long enough.

What do you think, boy? Is tonight the night? I think so, you big goofy puppy. Tonight's the night I'm going to ask Kathy to marry me. If you think she's going to say yes, speak.

Good boy!

I think she's going to say yes too. You're not jealous are you? No, of course you're not. You're always going to be my favorite. Kathy loves you too, ya know. Oh, I know she has a cat, but we're not going to let that stupid cat in this house, are we boy? No we're not! Just don't tell Kathy. Okay? Good boy! Cats get lost ALL the time, right boy? Yes they do!

Okay, come here. Sit. Give me paw. Good boy. Okay, both paws now. We're going to dance now. Good boy!

Dance with me … come on and be my partner, can't you see … I know boy, that was a stupid song, but I'm feeling pretty stupid now myself. Okay, boy, I'm heading out now, wish me luck.

Good boy!

Come here Buster. I don't know why Papa was so mean to me. I hate Papa. All I did was scare Emily. It wasn't a big deal. She's just a big baby, stupid girl. Everything she does is okay, but I do the littlest thing and I get sent to my room. Papa loves Emily more than me. Come up on the bed Buster. Good boy. Lie down. I said lie down! You want me to spank you like Papa spanked me? I will, I will spank you if you're a bad boy. I hate Papa. I'm never gonna watch TV with him again. I'll show him. Doesn't matter, because you love me more than you love Papa, right, Buster?

I knew you did.

You're a good boy, Buster.

Just like me.

You've been a perfect girl. From the time you were a puppy, you were so smart. And you're still our baby.

Give Daddy a kiss. Good girl. Okay, now you have to listen to me. Your Mommy is very sick. She's in bed upstairs, and she has a hard time coming down the stairs. Daddy's been sick too. I forget. I forget so much. I forgot to feed you yesterday morning. Mommy reminded me, but she couldn't come feed you because she just, she can't get out of bed anymore.

I wish you could have seen us when we were young. Give Daddy another kiss. Oh, when we were young.

You know all those cars in the garage? Well, Daddy bought them when they were nothing but wrecks, and Mommy and

Daddy, we put them together and made them all shiny just like they were brand new. Daddy was a pilot. I used to fly the big planes.

I don't want to forget that. I don't want to forget what it was like to be in the clouds, and look over at Mommy and see her smiling face, wearing that white scarf she loved so much, her beautiful hair. Mommy was very beautiful. Now, my baby, now Mommy's so skinny. I don't want to forget what Mommy looked like. Sometimes I do.

I met Mommy at the airport. I was a pilot. Did I say that? I was a pilot, and Mommy, she worked behind one of the ticket counters and the moment we saw each other we knew. Oh the adventures we went on. We went all over the world. That's when airplanes still had propellers.

We never had no kids. Just our Danes. Just our big beautiful fawn Great Danes. There was Tia, Elizabeth, Lady, Athena, oh, I'm forgetting one. I don't want to forget. I don't want to forget a single one. You were all our kids you know. Never talked back, nothing but love. Nothing but kisses. And we'd run in the backyard. Oh we'd run, and your Mommy would run. But that was long before you. We can't run any more.

We can't, we can't, well, we just can't do much of anything anymore.

It was always the three of us you know. Mommy, Daddy, and our baby. Give Daddy another kiss.

Well, I just wanted to make sure you knew how much we loved you, knew how much we loved each other. See baby girl, we can't go on any more. We can't have another tomorrow, because tomorrow might be the day I forget everything. Maybe tomorrow I forget to take care of Mommy like I should, or maybe tomorrow I forget to feed you and Mommy forgets to remind me.

And baby, I can't forget anymore. It hurts to forget. It hurts so much, because the one thing I always remember is what I was, what Mommy was. So baby, that's why Daddy and Mommy decided that there'll be no more tomorrows.

Give Daddy one more kiss baby. Good girl, good baby. I'm sorry baby, you deserve more tomorrows, but we need you to go with us. It's not your fault baby, and it's not going to hurt. I promise baby, it's not going to hurt you for even one second. You're going to go right to sleep. I'm just going to pull this little lever.

See? Aww, baby, that's so cute. I'm going to tell Mommy how you kissed the gun like it was one of your toys. Mommy's going to smile when she hears that. That's my good baby. My baby's not afraid. And my baby will never have to get old, and get arthritis, and be dependent on strangers.

Good night, my baby. Mommy and Daddy love you, and we'll see you in a few minutes.

NOOOO! I don't want to get up.

Just a few more minutes. OW, your nails hurt. Get your nose out of my face. NOOO. Stop with the kisses, I want to sleep a little bit. I said STOP WITH THE KISSES. Oh, you rotten girl. No, I don't care if you want to go outside, I'm the Daddy here.

No, no, no, no, no.

COME ON! That tickles! Please stop, Go away. I said go away!

Please. Please! Please?
Oh, all right, you win.

(Sung to the tune of The Supremes' *Baby Love*)
Doggy love, my doggy love, I walk you, Oh how I walk you!
And all you do is make me glad. Make me glad and your tail you wag.
Why you do me like you do. After all I feed to you. So deep in love with you
Doggy! Doggy! Doggy!
Doggy love, my doggy love ...

> *If I have any beliefs about immortality, it is that certain dogs I have known will go to heaven, and very, very few persons.*
> James Thurber

CHAPTER NINETEEN

ANATOMY OF A MURDER

Days passed into weeks, and weeks into months. I'd heard rumors of the Great White Tail, but had not seen it with my own eyes. During one of our walkies, Dexter, an aged and infirm Lab who lived a block away from us, told me that he'd seen the Great White Tail bounding through his yard a few weeks earlier. "Are you sure it was her," I asked. "Be the Tail you're searching for one with a scar across it's side?" he responded. "Aye," I replied. "That scar be from the fence that saved its worthless and evil life," I replied.

Ishmael, a tan and white collie, said that it had run across his front lawn just the day before. I was getting closer.

Then came the day I'd been waiting for.

It was a hot summer day, early August. It seemed that every block had two or three rabbit holes, all worth investigating of course, but to that point, none had yielded the Great White Tail. As I neared yet another area of disturbed Kentucky Blue Grass, I caught whiff of an odor so distinctive, so etched in my senses that it could mean only one thing; the Great White was close. I slowed my walk to a crawl, each paw treading so delicately that not even an earthworm would be aware of my approach. Right front paw and left rear, left front paw and right rear. I caught a break, in that my human had ambled ahead, the extension leash he now led me with allowing me just enough room to maneuver as freely as I needed.

The scent was stronger now and unmistakable. It was her.

I was within a foot of the ground that had been hideously violated in the cavalier way that rabbits do. I dropped to my stomach, quietly, in veritable slow motion. My focus was total, I was poised, I was ready to pounce at the slightest movement. And that's when I first heard the elfin squeaks.

Babies.

There were babies in that hole. It was despicable! That horrid hare was using babies to shield herself from potential attack. I could see it now, just as I would thrust my snout into her lair, she would send a horde of babies out from within, assuming I would be distracted enough to lash out at one of them, giving her just enough room for escape. But not now, not this time. No Earthly force was going to prevent me from my moment of victory.

And sure enough! No sooner had the thought crossed my mind when a veritable eruption of furry critters spewed forth from the hole. Squealing in terror, they scattered, running madly in every direction. Every instinct in my body begged me to give chase. They could have easily been caught and destroyed, but I did not give in to my baser instinct. I freely admit that this had nothing to do with mercy or pity, it had everything to do with the mayhem I wished to visit on the accursed Great White Tail.

Seconds passed like minutes, and then, as if in a vision, she appeared. It was her misfortune that when she surfaced, she had her back to me. At that point, it was all a blur, and I acted on nothing but adrenaline.

I lunged, catching her by surprise, her neck fitting perfectly between my incisors. One shake of my head, then a second, and her body went limp.

"Ruby!"

I did not try to hide my crime.

"Ruby, oh my God, Ruby. No! No!"

We made eye contact, my human and I.

"Drop it. Ruby drop it!"

I did.

And I smiled.

During the rest of the walkie home, my human hectored me and lectured me. He did not realize that there are simply some instincts in the animal kingdom that must be served. Preferably with some Fava beans and a nice Chianti.

As summer's brilliant yellows faded into the golds and browns of the Midwestern autumn, I noticed a slight change in my human. I picked up smells from another human, one I had not met. He was gone from home for longer periods of time, and upon his return would either be tremendously upbeat or frighteningly morose. It was the down times that had me worried. I'd heard stories from other canines about humans who would opt to end their own lives, an option no canine could even conceive. By this time, we'd had many months together, a growing history, and I'd come to really like him. There were even some days when, if prodded, I might have admitted to loving him. *Might* have. So I was troubled, and decided to be as attentive as possible.

One night, he came home especially late. It was never like him to leave me for more than five hours at a time. By hour seven, I was panicking. I began pacing throughout the house, all sorts of scenarios racing through my head. What if he was in a car accident? Would anyone know to come see about me? How would I eat? How long was I supposed to hold my bladder? Finally, I heard the car pull up outside. Nine hours!

Nine hours alone. If I hadn't been so worried, I'd have been furious. I did not wait at my customary spot at the top of the stairs, my kidneys screaming for release, reminding me that every second counted. So I positioned myself in the foyer, inches from the front door. My human came into the house through the garage door, and I wagged my tail furiously to convey my joy at seeing him. "Hi Baby," he said weakly. "You love me, Ruby girl, don't you?"

Yeah, yeah I love you, now open the Dog-damned door. It's been nine freakin' hours.

"Give me kisses."

ANYTHING YOU SAY! NOW OPEN THE DOOR!

Out we went, and I relieved myself almost immediately in the patch of grass directly in front of the house.

"Oh, my poor girl. I was a bad Daddy to you. I left you home too long. I'm sorry, pretty girl."

Damn right, now come on, let's go for a walkie. We went around the cul-de-sac, the night air cool. It was pitch black, the latest I think we'd ever been outside. It was dead silent, the only sounds those of my paws and his shoes making contact with the sidewalk. As we turned at the end of the block to U-turn our way back home, there was another sound, one I'd never heard before. It was sort of a muffled groan, then a distinctive sniffle, followed by more of the same. I turned back, and my current human was rubbing his eyes with his free hand. This marked the first time I'd seen a human really cry.

When we got back to the house, he stepped through the doorway before me, a first for that. He sat on the bottom stair, and I followed him. Unleashing my collar, he held my face with both of his hands and stared at me.

"You love me, Ruby? Ruby baby, you do love me, right? See, sometimes I don't know. I've been good to you, baby dog. I take you on good walkies, and I give you good food, and you go seepie in my bed. But sometimes I think you don't love me like most dogs love their Daddies. And Ruby, tonight, I need to be sure. See Ruby, I don't think anyone else loves your Daddy. Your Daddy loved somebody else but they don't love your Daddy. That's what they told me tonight, Ruby baby. So you see my beautiful girl, I really need you to love me."

He was still holding my head in his hands, so I reached out and gave him a swipe of my tongue.

"Thank you for the kisses, Ruby. Thank you very much. Now come on girl, I give you cookie and we go seepies."

I followed him up the stairs. He moved slowly, like he was wounded. True to his word, he gave me a cookie, then went right into the bedroom and lay down, not even bothering to undress. He lay on his back, staring at the ceiling. Every so often, a shudder of sadness quaked through his body. I sat on the floor at the side of the bed, transfixed. I didn't know what to do, so at first, I did nothing. Through the darkness, I could see that his eyes were wide open, moisture spilling down his cheeks. He made no effort to wipe his face, his eyes seldom blinking.

"Oh Ruby, why?"

My heart was breaking for him. I thought about all he'd done for me. I could have ended up so much worse off. I mean, what did I have to complain about? No yard? Okay, get over it. He took me for more walkies than I could handle. I had free rein of the house, could sleep wherever I wanted, eat almost as much as I wanted. And what did he ask in return? Don't crap on his carpet. That was about the extent of it.

As instinctively as I'd chased down that accursed rabbit, I suddenly knew what I had to do.

I leapt up onto the bed, and walked around to the far side of his prone figure. I stared down at him now, his eyes still fixed on the ceiling, the trail of water gleaming along his face as specks of moonlight streamed in through the window. I took a step closer to him, my right front paw making contact with his right arm. I took one last look and lay down, resting my head on his arm, looking right at his face. He turned towards me, and smiled through his pain.

"My baby, thank you. You do love me."

I did.

And I do.

> *Ever consider what they must think of us?*
> *I mean, here we come back from a grocery*
> *store with the most amazing haul—chicken,*
> *pork, half a cow. They must think we're the*
> *greatest hunters on Earth.*
> Anne Tyler

CHAPTER TWENTY

DOGS FOR THE ETHICAL TREATMENT
OF HUMANS

That's right, DETH. Now while I object to being referred to as a "dog" on religious grounds, I'll make an exception this time, because the acronym isn't as memorable if our group is called Canines for the Ethical Treatment of Humans. CETH just doesn't resonate with the same buzz as DETH. And lord knows with the limited attention span you humans have, any trick we can use to get you to focus is a good thing.

What is DETH? DETH is an organization dedicated to improving the treatment that humans bestow on other humans. While there are more than your share of humans who treat us canines despicably, the number of humans who treat other humans even worse pales in comparison. Hence, the need for DETH.

DETH, a canine concept, has been around since nearly the beginning of time, just like that human invention, murder. The basic tenet of DETH can be found in almost all human religious writing. "Do unto others as you would have them do unto you." PLEASE PAY ATTENTION: *"As you would have them do unto you."* It's not the prostituted form of that key expression of morality, not the way many twist it to justify a proliferation of violence and the Neanderthal "eye for an eye" mentality by misquoting it as, "Do unto others as they do unto you."

How can you tell if a canine is a member of DETH? Pay close attention to the canines you know. See how they treat you.

Does yours greet you with total unvarnished joy? Probably a member of DETH. Does yours show you what you perceive to be unconditional love? Probably a member of DETH. Forget to feed your canine, leave him home too long, maybe even strike him, only to find that he reacts by covering you with kisses? DETH in action. Does your canine's face make it impossible for you to suppress a smile? That's DETH. In the winter, does your canine curl up at your feet and keep them toasty? DETH again. When you cry, is the one living creature who does not leave your side until you feel better a canine? DETH.

If only you humans didn't need to be constantly reminded of how much better your quality of life would be if you lived with the very same ethos as that of the members of DETH. But it's too pie-in-the-sky to hope for you two-legged types to learn your lessons about the futility of war and the stupidity of my-religion-is-better-than-yours. I guess that means we canines will have to settle for knowing that we did our part, that we set the right example. What's the saying? You can lead a human to water …

🐾 🐾 🐾

- Did you ever notice how the same people who don't believe that global warming is a real threat also don't believe in evolution.
- A canine has never voted for a Bush. We have better uses for them.
- Red States are red because they're embarrassed, blue states are blue because there are too many red states.
- The difference between canines and people? The only

waste canines produce is biodegradable.
- Republicans are steadfastly against government intrusion into the private lives of citizens, unless it concerns a woman's uterus and a man's anus.
- Democrats make better ex-presidents than presidents.

I was born in 2003. For most of my life, the only American president I've known is George W. Bush. If I were unable to know history, here's what I would assume the US stood for:

1. Attacking countries that didn't attack us, but might some day.
2. Not attacking the guy responsible for attacking New York is okay, because he's a harder target to hit than a country that didn't attack us, but might some day.
3. The geography of death is more important than death itself. Apparently it's okay if 3000 Americans die in Iraq, not okay if they die in New York.
4. The rich are better than the poor because they need less help.
5. The religious are better than the non-religious because they say so.
6. Compassionate conservative is an oxymoron.
7. Being addicted to drugs is a crime but being addicted to alcohol is not.
8. The Democratic Party is so afraid of being seen as weak that it is weak.
9. If gays and lesbians are allowed to marry, heterosexuals will have to have their marriages annulled (and certain

evangelists and right wing politicians won't have any excuse to be ashamed of who they really are anymore).

10. Dick Cheney is the king.

Around the time I was writing this, there was quite a dust-up in the news about professional football player Michael Vick. Seems this multi-multi-multi-millionaire sponsored dog fighting in an area behind one of his palatial estates. (This sponsor of murder-for-sport has a palatial estate, and I don't have a yard! Where's the justice?) Against all logic, there were actually people out there defending Vick, because "the culture he grew up in has a different relationship with dogs than many other cultures in the United States."

Of course, that's nothing but rationalization of the lowest order.

Just because a wrong exists, doesn't make it any more right because people are used to it. Ironically, that was the very same logic used by the Old South to explain away their justification of slavery. Can't you just hear that folksy Foghorn Leghorn accent intoning, "The culchuh we all live in has a different relationship with the Nigra than you all do in the North."

I'll quote another southern accent in rebuttal.

"Stupid is as stupid does."

If I've offended any readers out there, I'm sorry. I'm not sorry *sorry* like I apologize. I'm sorry that you have so much trouble with reality.

Man is dog's idea of what God should be.
Holbrook Jackson
Dog is this man's idea of what God should be.
Tom Adrahtas

CHAPTER TWENTY-ONE

COOKIES FORTUNE

As I write this, Miss Ruby is curled up and fast asleep, snoring, her snout resting on my left foot, her butt perched on my right foot. I presume she's exhausted because we've just spent a good ten minutes playing fetch with the new toy I bought for her today. When it comes to toys in general, Ruby "don't play." When I bring home a new squeaky toy, it usually captures her attention for about three minutes, and once bored, she does not touch it until she needs to use it to signal her desire for another cookie. The "toy ruse" is just one of the weapons in her treat-seeking arsenal. In the matter of cookies, Ruby is both resourceful and relentless in her approach. I cannot blame her, as I am intimately familiar with the hell of addiction. It is painful to admit this weakness of mine publicly, it is even more painful to recount the sordid details. But for the benefit of the greater good, I shall do so.

You see, on 15 September of this year, I will have marked twenty-two years of being Oreo-free.

To say I had a problem with those sinful creations would be the definition of understatement. As a child, I was always overweight, but it was only after I first sampled Nabisco's crowning creation that I began to grow to the proportions that made Jenny Craig a rich woman. It started innocently enough with three cookies and a glass of ice-cold milk after I'd gotten home from fourth grade. By my junior year in high school, it was an entire row from a bag. Left to my own devices in college, it got really ugly. I'd become a varsity athlete by that time, a hockey goalie. The necessity for quickness and agility made me undertake a fitness regimen that I adhered to almost maniacally when it came to the weight room, on-ice training and riding the bike. I changed all of my eating habits as well. All except one. Gone were the greasy burgers and fries, replaced with chicken, fish and salads. I dropped nearly fifty pounds, looked good and felt great. But for all the positive changes, the one thing I could not give up was the Oreo.

Because I was eating so healthily now, it made the Oreo addiction worse. I was now able to rationalize that I could eat more of the cookies because I was more active than ever, and was eating hardly any fat in any other part of my diet. So I did eat more—and more and more. I hid a bag under my dorm room bed, and after the lights were out, my hand would reach down, nearly on its own, and fish out one last cookie. And maybe just one more.

My friends and teammates would hit the bars on Saturday night after our games, but I always found an excuse to go back to my dorm room, where I would put away a full bag, dipping them in a half gallon of ice- cold milk. I took great solace in the mind-altering sugar high which left me in a blissful place. At my worst, I was supporting a four-bag-a-week habit, which ruined me financially. I was reduced to panhandling on street corners, immediately spending my ill-gotten gains on another bag. All I could think about was my next fix. When the money was gone, I resorted to stealing. (Thankfully, I never had to sell my body. Not that I didn't want to, but I knew that if prostitution were my sole source of income, I'd likely never be able to afford another cookie.) I'd fill a grocery cart with food, and approach the checkout lines. I'd scout out the cashiers and the baggers carefully, always looking to get in the line with the most elderly cashier and the most handicapped bagger. Once I'd chosen a line, I made sure that my bags of Oreos were the last items checked. Inevitably, the cashier would be concentrating on ringing up all of the groceries (this was in the days before bar codes), and the bagger would be conscientiously stowing the items in the paper bags (before plastic was an option). As soon as I saw that both of them were completely lost in their work, I would grab the Oreos and run.

Knowing that neither could give chase, I usually only had to get a block or two before I could relax and enjoy my bounty. Once a safe distance away, I would tuck myself in next to some dumpster, tear open the bags, and get lost in the comfort and warmth of the sustenance the sugar provided.

I lived like that for months. I thought I was fooling my friends who kept asking me why my teeth were always so black, and where I was when they were going out doing normal harmless college stuff like binge drinking and date raping. They knew something was up, but I was not ready to admit my Oreoholism.

Eventually, I broke down. It is said that an addict must hit rock bottom before he can really get meaningful help, and for me that was certainly true. Once cocaine users cross into rock cocaine, hitting bottom is inevitable. Same holds true for those who favor LSD and turn to heroin.

For me, it was Double Stuff.

Yes, I'll never forget the day when I tried my first bag. I wasn't even working my grocery store scam. I happened to be in a 7-11. I wasn't even jonesing yet. I hadn't planned on walking down the cookie aisle. But somehow, I did. I was drawn there, so pathetic was my total lack of self-control. I knew there were Oreos in stock, and the animal instinct took over. As I reached for the comfort of the clear bag with the distinctive blue printing, my eyes caught sight of a bag with cool pink lettering. I thought I was hallucinating at first. There, right in front of me, was a cookie whose white center was twice as big as a normal Oreo. It couldn't be! It was too good to be true. As with all addicts, I rationalized. See, I thought with twice the white center, I would only need half my normal number of cookies to reach my own personal level of Nirvana. And also as with all addicts, all I did was eat twice as many.

So I OD'd.

Yes, I Oreo doubled.

As it turned out, I was one of the lucky ones. A friend happened upon me, passed out, smiling and giggling, face down in a fetid alley behind a Wal-Mart, my left hand still clutching an empty Double Stuff bag. I was rushed to the emergency room where I was told it took nurses three hours, a pliers, four wrenches, and a bottle and a half of Astroglide to get me to release the grip I had on that bag.

I was in rehab for weeks. They tried to get me to go cold turkey but I almost died in the process. So they weaned me, first with Hostess Cup Cakes, then Salerno Butter Cookies. Two months later, I walked out of the sanitarium, clean and sober. And I have never had an Oreo since.

In our early time together, I taught Ruby that in order for

her to get a cookie, she had to sit and then give me paw. It was so cute. At any time of day, she would come up to me, nudge me, sit, and extend her right paw. I would respond with a "Good girl," and immediately fetch her the prize she so desired. When I noticed that she was asking a little too frequently, I upped the ante and included a "lie down" into the process. She picked that up right away, and of course I was a sucker for her theatrics. Seeing how much she loved her cookie, I added another method of procurement to her repertoire. I taught her that if she played "fetch," she could earn a treat as well. This she did, usually twice a day.

This continued until a trip to the vet. Placing her on the scale and seeing it register at forty pounds, my initial thought was, "Hm, their scale is broken." Then it hit me; this was classic transference. I could no longer indulge my cookie obsession, so I lived vicariously through poor, overweight Ruby. I determined immediately that the cookie feedings would be cut drastically.

Ruby was not pleased. But it was the right thing to do, so I resisted her charms, and as any dog lover knows, the greatest con artist in the world is a dog who wants food. I remained strong for a long time, until Ruby found a method for which I had no defense.

I was sitting on the couch watching (appropriately enough) *Weeds* on Showtime. Ruby hopped up beside me, and I was totally prepared to rebuff the very sit-paw-lie-down act that I had taught her. Indeed, she sat. I responded with a stern, "No, Ruby." She looked at me, those endearing brown eyes wide and yearning as could be, and then laid her head down on my chest, never once losing eye contact with me.

"No, Ruby." She did not move. I have never seen anything so

adorable, never felt so helpless in the face of such an irresistible force since I found myself face-deep in a bag of Double Stuff.

So I got up, walked to the kitchen and got her a cookie.

Naturally, now every night when I sit, relax and watch some TV, I can count on her latest method of manipulation, and she can count on its success. I'm seriously thinking of staging an intervention.

I understand why Ruby goes to the lengths she does. I understand her dexterity in getting what she wants. I've been there. I must confess that my experience has left me so empathetic to her desires that I have become an enabler. I know it, I'm ashamed, but I cannot help myself. You could say I love seeing this latest antic so much that I'm addicted.

Again.

Things that upset a Terrier may pass
virtually unnoticed by a Great Dane.
Smiley Blanton

CHAPTER TWENTY-TWO

THE CURSE OF FRANKENSTEIN

I would be remiss if I did not address a growing matter of concern in the canine community. For some years now, humans have been conducting grisly genetic experiments in an effort to produce canines that are more convenient to care for. The egocentricity of this practice is one of the most obvious examples of what is morally wrong with the human race.

This trait can be seen in miniature in matters of romance. How many thousands of inches of column space have been spent by Ann Landers, Dear Abby, et al., imploring people to understand that it's nuts to marry someone in the hopes that you'll be able to change them to better suit you some day?

Dear Abby,

My fiancé has cheated on me four times in the last two and a half months. The pain is unbearable, but he has a such a good heart and he swears it will never happen again. I know that his wandering eye won't be a problem once I marry him, and that with love and determination, I can help him change. My friends say to dump him, that he'll never change.

What should I do?

Signed,

Confused in Fresno

Dear Abby will then give her some straight-from-the-heart common sense answer about how he'll never change, to cut her losses, and work at moving on. But here's the answer I'd like to see:

Dear Confused in Fresno,

Have you ever read this freakin' column before? Don't you know that the body part you least have to worry about is his EYE? Have you ever heard of sexually transmitted diseases? Have you ever once seen in this column a single example of a cheating fiancé who didn't become a cheating husband? No you haven't! Now pull your head out of your ass and kick him to the curb. And if any more of you cement-headed morons out there write again about wanting to marry someone because you can change them, please call Dr. Phil and quit wasting my time.

This, in a nutshell, is how I see people who want to have canines that are basically made on spec. Apparently, not enough of you ever saw *Frankenstein*, or those of you who did have opted to ignore the lesson contained therein; don't screw with domains of creation that should have been left solely in the paws of Dog.

This story really starts in the 1970s in Australia. That's where a breeder (read: mad scientist) first began working to construct a new breed of canine that would combine the intelligence and lack of shedding of a Poodle with the loyalty and strength of a Labrador. The resulting offspring would come to be known as a Labradoodle, and Pandora's Box was opened, never to be sealed again.

Now that "designer dogs" have been loosed on the world, of course it is our canine nature to welcome them with open arms. After all, it wasn't their fault. But that does not make the heresy practiced by your Mengelese breeders any less offensive. Here, along with the Labradoodle, is what they have wrought:

The Schnoodle. The name sounds like some sort of Bavarian pasta. In reality, this is the inter-breeding of a Schnauzer and a Poodle. The goal, I am told, was to create a dog with the loyalty of a Schnauzer and the intelligence of the Poodle. Like the Labradoodle, the Schnoodle is purported to be hypoallergenic.

The Goldendoodle. This combination Golden Retriever and Poodle is supposed to shed very little and be particularly good with children.

The Cockapoo. Sounds like a bird to me. This is a mix between the American Cocker Spaniel and a Poodle. Unlike the others I've named, these are bred from the smaller poodles—toys or miniatures—much to the relief of female Spaniels.

The Yorkipoo. Can these names be any more demeaning? This is also a smaller canine, the combination of a Yorkshire Terrier and a Poodle.

The Puggle. This is the one I take most personally. This is a Pug/Beagle mix. The face of this "breed" is longer than a Pug's face, which means they are less prone to respiratory issues, and the legs are longer than a Pug's which means it's less prone to joint problems. Seems to me that this mix was effected to basically improve the Pug. What's in it for the Beagle?

🐾 🐾 🐾

And why stop there? Why not keep going with these outrageous mixes? Here are some more that are sure to be out there some day:

The Lab Rat. Rat Terrier and a Labrador.
The Air Cor. Airedale and a Corgi
The Bearded Belgian. Bearded Collie and Belgian Sheepdog
The Cattle Sheep. Australian Cattle Dog and American Sheepdog
The Chow Hound. Chow Chow and Bassett Hound
The Weimar German. Weimaraners and German Shepherds
The Working Stiff. Any working class canine and a Mastiff
The Brittany Shorthairs. Brittany Spaniel and German Shorthaired Pointers
The Pyrenees Mountains. Great Pyrenees and the Bernese Mountain dog
The Spitz Water. Finnish Spitz and Portugese Water Dog
The Bull Shit. Bulldog and a Shih Tzu
The Jack Shit. Jack Russell and Shih Tzu
The Great Shit. Great Dane and a Shih Tzu.

🐾 🐾 🐾

While I admit I may be too emotionally involved about this practice to be objective, there is one dangerous by-product of the popularity of these canines that cannot be disputed. Since they've made the scene, there's been a proliferation of puppy mills, a problem that didn't need to be expanded. I'm sure that if you had enough interest to read this book in the first place, you're aware of the problems posed by puppy mills. In case any of you out there are still uninformed, puppy mills are places where canines are bred for the sole purpose of financial gain, where puppies are shoddily cared for, where breeders (read: "mad scientists") basically force canines into having litters as soon as they are physically ready, and then repeatedly afterwards. The fruits of these mills are the dogs that inhabit dog-selling chain pet stores.

Rest assured, that if our paws could hold a picket sign, there'd be rings of canines around every Puppy Palace and Pets-R-Us across the country. Unfortunately, the practice is still ongoing, and besides raising awareness of the situation, there's little that can be done. I'm afraid this does not have a real high priority amongst human law enforcement. So until the day comes when we have the canine population more under control (is this the right time to throw out the Terrier Trojan suggestion again?), please think twice before patronizing one of these dens of iniquity.

I mean, think about the possibilities if the bootie were on the other paw. How would you like it if we canines had the power to cross breed you humans based on making your religions more palatable and easier to live with? Here's some of what I would come up with:

Jehovah'sscientists. The perfect blend of creationism and evolution, and no one needs health insurance.

Irishcathotology. Sinners do not go to hell, they spend a weekend with John Travolta.

Christianrightacostals. Because they still speak in tongues, no one will be able to understand what they're preaching. Everybody wins.

Shakerquakers. Save big bucks on utilities.

Southernbapislam. Try to breed a pit bull meaner than this combo, I dare you!

Bahaiatheist. They don't believe in everything.

Shiit-Jews. At last, a solution to the crisis in the Middle East!

> *He is your friend, your partner, your defender, your dog. You are his life, his love, his leader. He will be yours, faithful and true, to the last best of his heart. You owe it to him to be worthy of such devotion.*
>
> Anonymous

CHAPTER TWENTY-THREE

IT'S MY TURN

(As you may remember, Ruby agreed to let me have two chapters of my own. But she's asleep right now, so I'm going to get another one in. Bear with me.)

It's been four and a half years since I first laid eyes on the terrified little beagle mix cowering in the back of a cage at the Heartland Animal Shelter. During that time, I had some challenging health issues, went through a stressful job change, put my house up for sale, faced some sticky financial times, and experienced the ups and downs of a relationship or two. All the while, the one constant was Ruby.

It is not novel to write that there is nothing like the greeting a dog gives you when you get home after a long day at work. It is also not trite, because it is so true that this exquisite moment dog owners get to experience every day should never be taken for granted. If, as Alice Walker famously contends, that "I think it pisses God off if you walk through a field and don't notice the color purple," it must enrage him (or her) if we ever consider the love we get from these miraculous creatures as something mundane.

There has not been a day that's gone by when Ruby hasn't done something to make me laugh or make me feel like the most important living being in the world. I can see it in her eyes. She has a way of looking at me like she's just waiting for whatever comes next. It might be a walk, a treat, a meal, fetch, or a command.

It doesn't matter what "it" is, so long as it "is." That's why she lies patiently outside my office when I'm working, why she stares at me out the window when I pick up the mail, why she sits outside the bathroom door when I shower, and why she's so thrilled whenever I come home.

I think I was lucky to have adopted my first dog later in life. I think that perhaps if I'd been able to have a dog when I was young, I wouldn't have the finely developed sense of wonder and appreciation for every little thing Ruby does that absolutely amazes me. In the riches of my memory, I have stored many pictures of our time together, most that bring smiles, some that bring amazement, some that bring tears, all of which serve as constant reminders of the complexity and necessity of having love in your life.

I'd had Ruby for about four months when I had to take a weekend trip. It would be the first time we'd be away from each other. One of my former players, Kelly, who is like a son to me, lived nearby with his wife, and they both loved Ruby, so I left her in their care for two and a half days. They both love dogs, they're both totally responsible, and I knew Ruby would be safe. So why did I feel the need to call them twice a day to check up on her? Why did I smile so much when they described the way she inspected each room of their apartment so thoroughly before finding a comfortable spot on their couch. And why was I so bothered to find out that on that very first night, Ruby unabashedly hopped up on their bed and slept with them? Why too was I so conflicted about picking her up late that Sunday? I was filled with the need to see this precious creature who had so won my heart, and I was absolutely stunned by how much I missed her, and how much I hated going to sleep without the reassuring feel of her warmth against my feet.

But I was also really apprehensive about how Ruby was going to react to seeing me. I desperately wanted her to go bonkers the moment she saw me, providing the proof I wanted that I was loved, but given her personality and her background, I prepared myself for a cool reception. I assumed that she'd resented being dropped off somewhere and forced to learn a new environment.

Kelly lived in a first floor apartment with a sliding glass door, and after parking the car, I made my way to their place, stopping outside and looking in through the window. He and his wife were sitting on the couch, Ruby sprawled out asleep on the floor a few feet away. I tapped at the glass, and Ruby's ears perked up, she turned, looked up at me, and slowly started to get to her feet. It was dark out, and my mind's defenses quickly conjured up the lack of light as the reason her reaction was so staid. I opened the door and stepped in.

"Hi, baby girl," I said as I entered.

And with that, Ruby went nuts. She made a beeline towards me, jumped up repeatedly and yipped with doggy glee. I dropped to my knees to give her a hug, and she smothered me in kisses. I have had a life that has given me many joys, but that moment was particularly exquisite. Over our first months together, Ruby had always been pretty reserved in all of her reactions. This was the first time she looked at me like she was so happy she simply couldn't contain herself. It was also the first time I really felt that I'd been "worthy."

That was the color purple.

We were on our usual neighborhood walk one day when Ruby spotted a squirrel just up ahead. It had the remnants of a sizeable green apple in its mouth, and stopped dead in its track the moment it sensed Ruby's presence. Ruby assumed a pointer's position; head lowered into a straight line with her spine, tail rigid and extended straight back, right leg curled up and off the ground. For nearly a minute, both creatures eyed each other intently, and for them nothing else existed in the world. Then came an explosion of action. Ruby lunged and the squirrel raced up a nearby tree, the apple still clenched tightly in its teeth. The squirrel settled about fifteen feet above us, Ruby now barking like a crazed seal, standing on her back paws, her front legs leaning up against the tree, making little jumping motions as if climbing that tree was a legitimate option. Apparently I was the only part of this threesome that recognized that option as a non-starter, because the squirrel, in its fright stemming from this apparent possibility, dropped the apple in its rush to gain position in a higher branch. In the process, Ruby learned what Newton had centuries earlier about gravity, and the apple hit her squarely between the eyes.

She shot me a glance that would have done any sitcom actor executing a double-take proud, and was clearly unhappy that I found this to be one of the funniest things I'd ever seen.

That was the color purple.

🐾 🐾 🐾

I woke up once in the middle of the night, to find that Ruby was asleep, her head resting on my neck. I had to use the washroom somewhat urgently, but refused to move for fear that I'd wake her up. After several minutes, I moved as slowly as possible to try and mitigate how much I might be disturbing her. My movement was met with a disapproving groan. When I returned to bed, she had managed to sprawl herself out across both pillows in such a way that I had about eight inches of room between the edge of the bed and her body. So instead of moving her, I simply wedged myself into that tiny area and pretended that I'd be able to sleep.

That was the color purple.

When I am sitting watching television, I find it nearly miraculous that Ruby has the run of the house, can sleep anywhere she wants, but most often chooses to sidle up right next to me.

That is the color purple.

I have an enormous king-sized bed, and if I leave a pair of sweats or a shirt on it, Ruby always opts to lie on top of the clothing. I choose to believe that this is a reflection of how much she loves me.

That is the color purple.

When Kelly and his wife moved to a new home about thirty minutes away, I'd lost my dog sitters. A weekend trip was upcoming, so I did research on boarding kennels. I saw two that I thought would be fine, but hated the thought of leaving Ruby at a kennel, especially given that she'd been a shelter dog. I opted to have her stay at the kennels operated by her vet. It was just minutes from my place, they had all of her medical records, and it felt safe. When I picked her up, her bed had been chewed up so badly it looked like a beaver had gotten to it. She was happy to see me, but she clearly communicated that this place was not going to do.

For the next trip I opted for kennel choice #2. It was run by a very warm woman with an English accent. The kennels were larger than my vet's were, it was less cramped, and I had a good recommendation on it from a friend. "Now don't look at Ruby after I take her leash," the nice lady said. "I'm going to lead her back to her kennel quickly so she won't know you're gone right away."

Having character no stronger than Lot's wife, I immediately looked at Ruby as she was being led away. She turned back at me with a pleading look of abandonment that tore me up.

I'm fifty-one years old, a hockey coach, and been through a lot. I'm here to tell you that I could never face that look again. That's why Ruby now has a stay-overnight-at-my-house dog sitter any time I need to be out of town.

And even that's the color purple.

I was never a morning person. For me, getting up early meant breakfast at nine, the end result of late night coaching hours and film review. That's different now.

Now, my favorite time of day is 6:15 AM. Every morning at that time, I detect a pair of large brown eyes staring at me. Sometimes they are looking down at me, sometimes when I open my eyes for the first time that day, they are inches from mine. Ruby interprets the slightest movement by me as a signal to her that it's time to wake me up. Thus, she begins her routine.

It usually starts with poking her nose into my hand. When that doesn't elicit enough movement for her liking, she moves into phase two, which is lightly executed kisses to my nose. This tactic is impossible to ignore, so when I move my face away from her as a reaction, she turns her back to me, and throws herself, spine first, into my side, a move that would do any professional wrestler proud. Of course there is method to this particular madness, because she always throws her weight at me from the side that's closest to the wall. At the same time, she'll dig her paws into the bed and begin nudging me away from the wall and towards the edge of the bed, physically positioning me to either wake up, get up, or fall off the bed. For good measure, she'll occasionally utter a sort of whispering version of a bark, as if she knows it's too early to emit the full-throated version, but needs to make a verbal statement to reinforce what she's doing physically.

Genius, I tell you.

I love the morning. And that can only be the color purple.

Dogs fill as many roles in their human interactions as they fill voids. They are the eyes of the blind, extensions of law enforcement, comfort for the infirm, ranchers, hunting companions and protectors of the home. Their value to human society cannot be objectively measured. But the level of their worth cannot now, and never has been judged by their capacity for work. Because the single biggest asset they represent is what I can attest to first hand.

Unlimited love.

I did not say "unconditional" for a reason, and I will let Ruby address that in the concluding chapter. I said unlimited, and that's what I meant.

I have been alone for many years. I had work that I found eminently fulfilling. I've known the incomparable highs of National Championships and the stinging losses of agonizing defeats in that work, and learned along the way that pain is often a more masterful teacher than success. I have been surrounded by a lifetime's accumulation of wonderful friends, a surrogate family of choice more true than those many are born into. I have not accumulated much material wealth along the way as it was never a priority, a trait I was once very proud of, but one that, now on the other side of fifty, I am reconsidering as a bit too flippant.

Through all of it though, I have spent most of my life most comfortable being alone. I have lived alone since I was in my early twenties, and came to love the independence of that state, the ability to go when I wanted to go, stay when I wanted to stay, not have to be nice if I was feeling surly, not having to meet anyone half way when I could have it all my way. It was a selfish way to live. I've always admitted that, and felt pretty good about not prioritizing or expecting an intimate relationship because of that selfishness.

Enter Miss Ruby.

Now I know that I need to be home because someone else demands it, now I know what it is to care about another living creature so much that *not* having me as *the* priority anymore

feels like life's greatest gift.

And that is truly the color purple.

Money will buy you a pretty good dog,
but it won't buy the wag of his tail.
Anonymous

CHAPTER TWENTY-FOUR

WHAT'S UNCONDITIONAL LOVE GOT TO DO WITH IT?

So who am I to talk about love? I'm a canine, and no one knows more about love than we do.

You humans are fond of saying that dogs give unconditional love. That's not true, and that observation is more damning of your species than you can possibly admit. Our love is *not* given unconditionally. It is given to anyone who deserves it. The most basic difference between you and us is that *we* know that more people deserve love than *you* opt to recognize. There are very few people out there who don't deserve to be loved, and folks, my suspicion is that's why Dog created canines in the first place.

Not only to provide love, but to remind you lesser species about the true power and joy that love brings.

Now give me a cookie.

If there are no dogs in heaven, then when I die,
I want to go where they went.
Will Rogers

Tom Adrahtas lives in Chicago with Ruby.

ABOUT
TOM ADRAHTAS

Lover of dogs, comedy, Motown music and hockey, Tom Adrahtas has written an unauthorized biography of Diana Ross and the authorized biography of NHL goalie Glenn Hall. **Ruby's Humans**, his third book, gives him a unique mouthpiece to express his satiric take on popular culture. He lists Al Franken, George Carlin, Jonathan Winters and Gary Larson as comedic influences. He claims to love Ruby more than he loves himself.

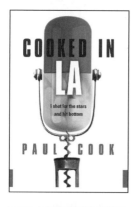

Cooked in LA ■ Paul Cook

How does a successful young man from a "good" home hit bottom and risk losing it all? *Cooked In La* shows how a popular, middle-class young man with a bright future in radio and television is nearly destroyed by a voracious appetite for drugs and alcohol.

Non Fiction/Self-Help & Recovery | US$ 24.95
Pages 304 | Cloth 5.5" x 8.5"
ISBN 978-1-60164-193-9

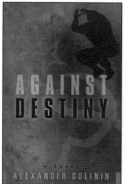

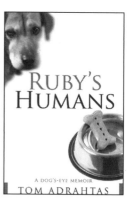

Against Destiny
■ Alexander Dolinin

A story of courage and determination in the face of the impossible. The dilemma of the unjustly condemned: Die in slavery or die fighting for your freedom.

Fiction | US$ 24.95
Pages 448 | Cloth 5.5" x 8.5"
ISBN 978-1-60164-173-1

Let the Shadows Fall Behind You
■ Kathy-Diane Leveille

The disappearance of her lover turns a young woman's world upside down and leads to shocking revelations of her past. This enigmatic novel is about connections and relationships, memory and reality.

Fiction | US$ 22.95
Pages 288 | Cloth 5.5" x 8.5"
ISBN 978-1-60164-167-0

Ruby's Humans
■ Tom Adrahtas

No other book tells a story of abuse, neglect, escape, recovery and love with such humor and poignancy, in the uniquely perceptive words of a dog. Anyone who's ever loved a dog will love Ruby's sassy take on human foibles and manners.

Non Fiction | US$ 19.95
Pages 192 | Cloth 5.5" x 8.5"
ISBN 978-1-60164-188-5

The Unbreakable Child ■ Kim Michele Richardson

Starved, beaten and abused for nearly a decade, orphan Kimmi learned that evil can wear a nun's habit. A story not just of a survivor but of a rare spirit who simply would not be broken.

Non Fiction/True Crime | US$ 24.95
Pages 256 | Cloth 5.5" x 8.5"
ISBN 978-1-60164-163-2

Save the Whales Please
■ Konrad Karl Gatien & Sreescanda

Japanese threats and backroom deals cause the slaughter of more whales than ever. The first lady risks everything—her life, her position, her marriage—to save the whales.

Fiction | US$ 24.95
Pages 432 | Cloth 5.5" x 8.5"
ISBN 978-1-60164-165-6

Screenshot
■ John Darrin

Could you resist the lure of evil that lurks in the anonymous power of the Internet? Every week, a mad entrepreneur presents an execution, the live, real-time murder of someone who probably deserves it. *Screenshot*: a techno-thriller with a provocative premise.

Fiction | US$ 24.95
Pages 416 | Cloth 5.5" x 8.5"
ISBN 978-1-60164-168-7

KÜNATI

Kunati Book Titles
••••••••••••••••••••••••••••••
Provocative. Bold. Controversial.

Touchstone Tarot ■ Kat Black

Internationally renowned tarot designer Kat Black, whose *Golden Tarot* remains one of the most popular and critically acclaimed tarot decks on the market, has created this unique new deck. In *Touchstone Tarot*, Kat Black uses Baroque masterpieces as the basis for her sumptuous and sensual collaged portraits. Intuitive and easy to read, this deck is for readers at every level of experience. This deluxe set, with gold gilt edges and sturdy hinged box includes a straightforward companion book with card explanations and sample readings.

**Non Fiction/New Age I US$ 32.95 I Tarot box set with 200-page booklet I Cards and booklet 3.5" x 5"
ISBN 978-1-60164-190-8**

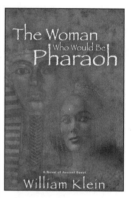

Sleepers Awake
■ Patrick McNulty

Monstrous creatures invade our world in this dark fantasy in which death is but a door to another room of one's life.

**Fiction I US$ 22.95
Pages 320 I Cloth 5.5" x 8.5"
ISBN 978-1-60164-166-3**

The Nation's Highest Honor
■ James Gaitis

Like Kosinski's classic *Being There, The Nation's Highest Honor* demonstrates the dangerous truth that · incompetence is no obstacle to making a profound difference in the world.

**Fiction I US$ 22.95
Pages 256 I Cloth 5.5" x 8.5"
ISBN 978-1-60164-172-4**

The Woman Who Would Be Pharaoh
■ William Klein

Shadowy figures from Egypt's fabulous past glow with color and authenticity. Tragic love story weaves a rich tapestry of history, mystery, regicide and incest.

**Fiction/Historic I US$ 24.95
Pages 304 I Cloth 5.5" x 8.5"
ISBN 978-1-60164-189-2**

KÜNATI

Kunati Book Titles
••••••••••••••••••••••••••••••
Provocative. Bold. Controversial.

The Short Course in Beer
■ Lynn Hoffman

A book for the legions of people who are discovering that beer is a delicious, highly affordable drink that's available in an almost infinite variety. Hoffman presents a portrait of beer as fascinating as it is broad, from ancient times to the present.

Non Fiction/Food/Beverages | US$ 24.95
Pages 224 | Cloth 5.5" x 8.5"
ISBN 978-1-60164-191-5

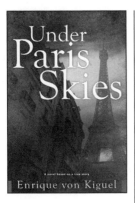

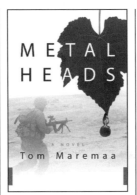

Under Paris Skies
■ Enrique von Kiguel

A unique portrait of the glamorous life of well-to-do Parisians and aristocratic expatriates in the fifties. Behind the elegant facades and gracious manners lie dark, deadly secrets

Fiction | US$ 24.95
Pages 320 | Cloth 5.5" x 8.5"
ISBN 978-1-60164-171-7

Metal Heads
■ Tom Maremaa

A controversial novel about wounded Iraq war vets and their "*Clockwork Orange*" experiences in a California hospital.

Fiction | US$ 22.95
Pages 256 | Cloth 5.5" x 8.5"
ISBN 978-1-60164-170-0

Lead Babies
■ Joanna Cerazy &
Sandra Cottingham

Lead-related Autism, ADHD, lowered IQ and behavior disorders are epidemic. *Lead Babies* gives detailed information to help readers leadproof their homes and protect their children from the beginning of pregnancy through rearing.

Non Fiction/ Health/Fitness & Beauty | US$ 24.95
Pages 208 | Cloth 5.5" x 8.5"
ISBN 978-1-60164-192-2